HIS CHRISTMAS LOVE SONG

ELLE WATERS

For Cat and Rose

ONE

JESSE'S WHISTLING when the bomb goes off.

He's been in a good mood ever since he realized he only has a month until his stint in the Peace Corps is up, and he'll be returning home. It's not that he hasn't loved his time in Southeastern Africa—it's been his home for nearly two years now. But he misses his family. His friends. He misses cheeseburgers. And his notebook is overflowing with song lyrics about missing them. Well, not the cheeseburgers. Though an ode to cheeseburger might make a good novelty tune.

He needs to go to home to Tennessee and work on new material if he's ever going to make it in the cutthroat world of country music.

He misses his guitar, too. He'd brought one with him to Malawi, but it had gotten stolen within forty-eight hours. Lesson learned. The first of many. He's loved his time working here—the people are endlessly welcoming, always appreciative of the medical care his team brings to them. He's gotten used to the food, and as repetitive as the meals sometimes are, he's grateful that they never have to worry about running out, not like some of the villagers in the places they go, where food isn't something you can go to a supermarket and buy.

Yeah, when he gets home he's going to go out for the biggest cheeseburger in Jackson, tune up his guitar, polish a dozen songs until they shine, and then he's going to Nashville. In the past two years he's dealt with malaria, snakes, and helped deliver six babies. How hard could it be to face down a record executive or two?

Ryan might be able to give him some pointers.

Jesse recognized him right away when he'd shown up with the most recent crop of volunteers. Jesse has been away from America for nearly two years, but Ryan Winslow had scored a top ten country hit long before that. "Cowboy Livin'" had been everywhere Jesse's junior year of college. None of Ryan's other songs charted as high, but Jesse still has the CD of Ryan's debut album, *Country Boy*, boxed away with the rest of his stuff in his mom's basement.

He loves Ryan's mellow voice, admires his range that can veer from twangy to rock-screamy depending on the song. And he loves the picture on the album cover—a black and white shot of Ryan almost in silhouette—all pillowy lips and long lashes, looking more like a pin-up model than a country singer.

It's a good look.

Ryan got a lot of attention at the time of its release for being one of the only out gay country stars, and Jesse, who's been firmly bi since making out with Kyle Drysdale at the winter formal senior year of high school, felt like maybe he could be out and get a record contract, too.

But then life happened. He played the only gigs he could get—weekend afternoons at the steakhouse where he was also a busser. He graduated college with a half-hearted degree in business and took EMT classes because no one was interested in the demo he made with some friends in a studio he paid for with his entire graduation money.

Right before he took a job as an EMT, someone mentioned the Peace Corps, that his medical training would be useful there. Two years without having to feel like a failure because his music dreams hadn't come true and where he could really help people? He signed up without a second thought.

He'd been so busy once he got here, learning the customs and the way the Peace Corps did things. He'd been too exhausted to think about his dreams deferred. But then he'd gotten the hang of it, gotten addicted to the buzz of helping people. Some days he has enough energy left over to think about the life he wants to have some-day, and he goes and adds more lyrics to his notebook.

A famous country musician showing up at camp had been a shock. He's younger than Jesse expected, for one thing. When Ryan's success had come early. He wasn't much older than Jesse's twenty-four. He might have been on the quiet side, but Jesse learned quickly that Ryan was there to work and roll up his sleeves like everyone else. He volunteered for the regular two-year stint, too, was in Ethiopia for a year before transferring here. Jesse didn't ask why a country star would leave the music scene for that long; it wasn't any of his business.

He and Ryan have talked a couple of times. They aren't friends or anything, but Jesse resolves that before he's on the plane home, he's going to ask Ryan for advice about breaking into the music business. And maybe for his autograph.

So yeah, he's whistling, content with things, looking forward to the future. That's when the SUV in front of the one he's riding in just kind of leaps into the air—the sound of the explosion comes a split second later.

Kim slams on the breaks. "Land mine," she yells. He can barely hear her over the ringing in his ears. Jesse's instantly in emergency mode. He leaps out of the SUV, taking inventory as he approaches the vehicle that was hit. It's still on its wheels, but there's smoke pouring from under the hood, black and thick; something's on fire. They have to get everyone out of the car. They were a two-vehicle caravan bringing supplies to a village three hours' drive away. Just a simple delivery. Kim, Moses, and him in the rear SUV, Diego and Ryan in the lead.

Moses is already out and gone for the fire extinguisher. Kim grabs the medical kit. Diego's gotten himself out of the driver's side of the damaged vehicle. His face is red—blood from a head wound. He probably has glass embedded in his skin, but he was wearing sunglasses, maybe that protected his eyes. But Ryan— Ryan's not getting out of the car. Jesse gets to the passenger door, tries the handle, but it won't budge. He can see Ryan through the window. His eyes are closed. He's not moving.

Jesse gives up on that door, goes to the back. It's locked. He remembers the glass breaker he has on his keyring, uses it to smash the back window, reaches inside, unlocks the door revealing boxes of supplies. He shoves them aside so he can reach forward and unlock Ryan's door. He doesn't look to see if Ryan's breathing. He opens the door carefully but quickly, unbuckles Ryan, pulls him free of the car.

There's another small explosion, and the flames engulf the car a dozen feet behind them.

Jesse pulls Ryan as far as he can toward the other SUV where he sees Kim examining Diego, who seems disoriented but on his feet.

He looks down at Ryan, cradled in his arms, almost afraid to check for a pulse. But his training kicks in and he puts him on his back, checks his vitals. He's breathing. His pulse is steady.

Jesse sucks in a harsh breath of relief when Ryan's eyes suddenly fly open, bluer than anything.

"There he is," Jesse says, smiling down at him. "Stay still. I'm gonna check you out."

"What happened?" Ryan's voice is weak.

"Small explosion. Diego's gonna be okay. You're gonna be okay." Jesse talks nonsense as he runs his hands over Ryan, checking for breaks and other injuries. He's got a goose egg near his temple. He must have smacked his head against the door or the window which caused him to lose consciousness.

"Bleeding," Ryan says.

"No, you've got a big bump, but you're not bleeding."

"No—you. Bleeding." Ryan's eyes dart to Jesse's arm.

He looks down at himself, feels a wave of dizziness as the pain finally registers. He is, in fact, bleeding. There's a chunk of sheet metal embedded in the back of his right bicep. He vaguely remembers feeling something glance off him during the second explosion, but he'd been so focused on Ryan he hadn't paid attention.

"Well, shit, you're right," he says.

Ryan struggles to sit, but Jesse puts his left arm out to keep him down. "Hang on. You need to stay put."

"Your arm—"

"I'm fine." Jesse blinks away dark spots that suddenly appear in his vision, or tries to. The world goes insistently gray, then black.

RYAN TALKS his way into the medical building with a practiced grin; he knows what effect his smile has on people. The building isn't very big, but it has strict security protocols. He gets a badge and has to scrub his hands and wear a mask.

He knows the drill from when he was here yesterday to visit Diego. He'd escaped with a bunch of cuts on his head from broken window glass, been patched up and pumped full of antibiotics and kept overnight. Ryan hadn't even been admitted. Once they got back to camp the doctor diagnosed him with a mild concussion and told him to rest. But Jesse's still here. They wouldn't let Ryan see him yesterday; he's not taking no for an answer today.

This is the nearest thing to a hospital for miles, and

he passes rooms that are full of people in various stages of need, cursing himself for a fool. He's such an idiot. He thought the Peace Corps would be an escape, a way for him to stop being himself for a little while. Turns out, he's still him when he's thousands of miles away from home.

He knows, intellectually, that he's contributed during his time here. He knows he's done some good. He also knows the vehicle he was riding in hitting a land mine isn't his fault. But it still seems like something that would happen to him. Ryan Winslow, second-rate country singer runs away from home looking for meaning, gets blown up.

He can't even do that part properly. He's fine, and Jesse, the kid who pulled him out of the car, the kid who saved his life, is stuck in here, recovering from emergency surgery.

He finds his way to the recovery room all right. Jesse's inside, talking to the same doctor who examined Ryan yesterday. He knocks on the door frame and they both look up. Dr. Moore's wearing a mask over his salt and pepper beard, but his eyes narrow at the sight of Ryan. Jesse, maskless, tries on a smile, but he looks pale, his normally light skin leached of all color, making his almost-black hair starker by comparison.

"Okay if I visit the hero for a minute?" Ryan asks.

"For a short minute," Dr. Moore says.

"How's the patient?"

"I just checked his sutures. No sign of infection. If we can keep it that way, Mr. Arlyn will be back on his feet in a few days."

"I'm fine," Jesse insists wanly. "It's just a cut on the arm."

"That piece of metal was embedded three inches deep. We had to do careful surgery to address the injury to the muscles. If you don't rest and let it heal properly, you could have lasting muscle damage," Dr. Moore says sternly.

"Jesus." Ryan hadn't known exactly why Jesse had been kept so long, but now he gets it. He'd lost a lot of blood, too. The ride back to base from the bomb site had been terrifying. Jesse had woken up a couple of times but hadn't been lucid. Ryan had held his arm steady, so the metal didn't knock into anything else, blood soaking his clothes, while Kim drove and Diego stanched his bleeding in the front seat. They'd faced a mountain of paperwork, too, once they were deemed stable.

"You're okay?" Jesse asks, turning to look at Ryan. "How's your head?"

"I'm good," Ryan says. "You saved my life."

Jesse smiles faintly. "It was a life worth saving." His voice sounds dreamy.

Ryan frowns and looks at Dr. Moore. "How many drugs is he on?"

Dr. Moore's warm brown eyes crinkle at the edges. "Enough to make him comfortable. You'll have to make it quick. I'll give you another minute."

"Okay."

Dr. Moore leaves and Ryan lets out a breath. "Listen, Jesse, I wanted to thank you. You really did save my life. The others told me that if you hadn't pulled me out of the car, I'd have been caught in the second explosion."

"Of course," Jesse says, sounding clearer, his gray eyes bright. "It wasn't a big deal."

"It was to me," Ryan says. "And I want you to know if there's anything I can ever do for you, here or back in the States, whatever, just say the word. Okay?"

Jesse's silent. He should let him rest. He starts to back out of the room, but Jesse says, "Well, there is one thing. I was going to ask you about this before, but, well. I write songs. Sing 'em, too, sometimes. Play guitar." He grits his teeth. "If this arm gets well enough to play again."

Ryan's sympathy at the idea of not being able to play guitar again wars with resentment at what Jesse's implying. Of course he'd come to Africa to escape from the music industry and end up meeting an aspiring singer-songwriter. He tamps down his irritation and reminds himself he offered. Jesse's just taking him at his word.

"Oh yeah? Well, when you're all better, send me something," Ryan finds himself saying.

"Seriously? Oh, that would be amazing. I will, I totally will," Jesse says, suddenly sounding perfectly cogent. "I have a demo that didn't go anywhere, but I've got about a million other songs. Some of 'em would be perfect for your voice."

It seems Jesse's given this some thought. What has Ryan gotten himself into?

"Well, uh. I'll take a listen." He pats the kid on his good arm.

Jesse's smile is brilliant. "Promise?"

What else can Ryan say? "Promise."

Jesse's smile morphs into a huge yawn. Ryan finds

himself smiling at Jesse's swift transformation into a sleepy puppy, eyes drooping and everything. "That's good. We're going to be so good together, Ryan. You'll see."

His chest tightens at Jesse's casual certainty. "I better go now."

Jesse blinks sleepily. "Ryan?"

"Yeah?"

"I'm glad you're okay."

Ryan can't explain the lump in his throat. He nods and hustles out of there before he can do something silly like cry.

TWO

SIX YEARS LATER

THE AUDIENCE'S applause reaches a crescendo as Ryan strums the first notes of their encore number, "Strawberry Smile." Jesse walks out of the wings carrying his guitar, sits on the stool that's waiting for him, and joins in. It's a duet, the first one they ever recorded together, and it's still his favorite. The audience goes crazy when they get to the chorus about "his strawberry lips and strawberry tongue," and Ryan's cheeks get a little red, the way they always do when he sings the line about making love all night long. It's a song about summer love, it's got a zippy little melody, and it's about a boy. It's also a fan favorite. More than one couple—same gender and not—have told them they used it as their wedding song.

The last notes die away, and they take their bows to an enthusiastic crowd. It's not a huge venue, but they sold it out three nights in a row, which is a feat for a country act way up here in Boston. It's the last night of their tour—endless weeks spent on the road. Jesse's exhausted, and he knows Ryan is too. They step off the stage and thank their crew, handing off their instruments to their trusted gear guys and gals, then hightail it to the dressing room.

"Great show," Jesse says, patting Ryan on the back. He's hot to the touch, sweat bleeding through his plain black T-shirt.

Ryan smiles back, but it doesn't quite reach his eyes. "You too, Jess."

If Jesse's been a little worried about his plan, now he's sure he's doing the right thing. Ryan needs the smile back in his blue eyes, and it's Jesse's job to put it there.

"So, Steph already brought the car over. Our stuff is packed. What do you say we just hit the road now? I'll drive."

Ryan whips his sweaty shirt over his head. "Why are we spending our first free week in ages taking a road trip again?"

"Well, it's not a road trip, exactly," Jesse hedges. He looks away from the broad expanse of Ryan's naked back and grabs a towel. He dries the sweat off the back of his neck and grabs a fresh shirt of his own. He'd been purposefully vague about their post-tour plans, not wanting Ryan to have time to gather reasons not to come.

Ryan pulls a clean tee over his head, runs a hand through his sweat-damp hair. He looks good, even with shadows under his eyes. He turned thirty-four on his last birthday and he's just starting to get some serious lines around the corners of his eyes when he smiles. The problem is, he hasn't been smiling enough lately. Cataloging Ryan's smiles is second nature now.

"If it's not a road trip, then what it is?" Ryan asks suspiciously.

"It's a three-hour drive and then we'll stop for the night. I already made sure we can check in late without a problem."

"We can check in *where* late?"

"It's going to be great," Jesse says. "It's a lodge with lots of little cabins, fireplaces, the works. It's in the middle of nowhere Vermont. It's going to be beautiful this time of year. Snow, and everything. We'll be able to unplug and think about the album."

Ryan grits his teeth. "I can't fucking believe I let you fucking talk me into doing a fucking Christmas album."

Jesse's not so sure Ryan isn't going to back out, which is why he wants to get some songs sketched out before the momentum disappears. "A Christmas album is the number one most requested thing from our fans. It's a slam dunk. And if we make progress this week, we might be able to put out a surprise single this very Christmas."

"That's like two weeks away," Ryan says, eyebrows raised.

"You know we can work fast when we're inspired. Come on, it'll be fun. We haven't written together in too long." They'd been too busy touring over the past year to do much in the way of writing.

"It's just that Christmas albums are so corny. Boring as hell, too."

"So we'll make ours edgy. Unexpected. Instead of mistletoe and reindeer, we'll sing about cacti and tarantulas."

That gets a laugh out of Ryan. Jesse's chest puffs

with pride. Making Ryan laugh never gets old, even after six years of working together, first as writing partners, then recording together, then performing, until now they're a package deal. Ryan still does solo shows sometimes, and Jesse's put out one solo album that was even nominated for a Grammy. This tour they'd been billed together, and it had been their best selling tour by far. Jesse owes everything he knows about the music business to Ryan and his endlessly patient manager, Sadie Darling, but he likes to think he's taught Ryan a thing or two as well. Sam seems to think so, anyway. After the first six months of shadowing Ryan when they got back the States, she'd taken Jesse aside and thanked him, not only for bringing Ryan safely home, but for bringing him back to music.

"All the industry bullshit was making him ready to quit. I almost couldn't blame him. But you've made him remember why he started in the first place. You've brought the joy back for him."

He had been astonished at her words. He'd basically felt like he was a thorn in Ryan's side since they got back. Not that Ryan had ever been rude or seemed like he wanted to take back the hospital room offer Jesse had shamelessly accepted. But he kept his feelings close to the vest. Jesse was pretty sure Ryan didn't hate him, but it wasn't until a few weeks after that conversation with Sadie that he let himself think that Ryan might actually like him. It was a late night in the recording studio working on Ryan's take on one of Jesse's songs. They were punch drunk and had finally nailed what would become their first big hit together. Ryan had slapped him on the shoulder, let out a bright, happy laugh.

"We got it! That's a good one. Good job, Jess." It was the first time he'd called him that.

After that night, they were friends. Six years later, Jesse could confidently say they were best friends.

But with all their success, with the memorable times they've had on the road and back home in Tennessee, there's still something missing. Jesse's mission is to make Ryan's happiness a priority. He knows Ryan has complicated relationships with the music industry, with fame, with the fans. He knows if it wasn't for him, Ryan might have bowed out a long time ago. But he also knows that Ryan loves making music. He loves to sing; he loves to play guitar. He loves performing to crowds who know every song in their repertoire so well they sing along to every word. Professionally, they've excelled. Which means that Ryan's life can really only use an upgrade in one more department.

Love.

In the last six years, Ryan has had exactly two relationships that lasted more than a night. Jesse's certain that if Ryan found the right guy to settle down with, maybe even start a family with, that would be the final part of the puzzle of his friend's happiness. The problem is, Ryan makes it really hard for Jesse to help him find a guy. In the last few months, he's completely stopped even going out for a drink with any of the eligible guys Jesse finds for him.

Jesse's been forced to take extreme measures.

"So it's just a Vermont lodge and we're just going to

do a writing session?" Ryan says, breaking into his thoughts. He tucks his water bottle into his bag, unplugs his phone charger from the wall.

"What else would it be?" Jesse asks defensively. He scrambles to make sure all his stuff is shoved into his travel bag.

"I just wouldn't put it past you to have some arranged marriage thing worked out. You know, like *90 Day Fiancé* or something."

"No weddings planned," Jesse says lightly. "But if you want to leave tomorrow in order to have a drink with Matt tonight, I'd be okay with that."

"Matt the venue manager?" Ryan asks, forehead crinkling. "Why would I want to do that?"

"Because he's single and nice and he thinks you're hot."

"He's met me three times. I'm not going for a drink with Matt."

"You wouldn't go for a drink with Michael either, or the super cute guy we met in New York, Mitch."

"Maybe you should stop setting me up with guys whose name starts with M," Ryan says, double checking the room for any forgotten items. "Or better yet, stop setting me up, period."

"Don't you want to meet someone?" Jesse asks. They've had a version of this conversation every few weeks for a year now. "It's been ages since you and Cameron broke up."

Ryan had dated Cameron Keane for six months or so while they were in Nashville for a long stretch recording their last album. Then Cameron had gone on tour in Europe and that was the end of it.

"If Matt and Michael and Mitch are so great, why don't *you* date them?" Ryan says, trotting out another of his go-to rebuttals.

"I'm doing fine." Jesse has never been at a loss for company when he wants it. He's perfectly happy with one- and two-night stands and friends-with-benefits situations. Ryan's the one who's built for monogamy, who will make an amazing partner and an incredible dad. But he'll never get to that stage with anyone if he doesn't even try.

"Well, then, so am I," Ryan says. "You don't need to worry about me."

"I can't help but worry about you, you know that. Ever since—" He rubs the scar on his right tricep nearly unconsciously. The scar is a reminder of how close he'd been to never knowing Ryan, to losing him before he'd gotten a chance to make the best friend he'd ever had.

"Yeah, yeah." The bitterness in Ryan's voice takes Jesse aback. "You know, sometimes I think you should have left me in the damn SUV."

"Don't say that." Jesse's stomach aches. He knows Ryan doesn't mean it, but it's still hard to hear. "Listen, we're both worn out from the tour. This break is going to be just what we need. We can catch up on sleep and work a little and by the time we head back to Tennessee for Christmas, things are going to be better."

Ryan sighs. He rubs his eyes, then puts on a small smile. "Sorry I'm such a downer. You're right. A little relaxation in the mountains sounds pretty good. And there'll be snow, right? No snow back home." His smile gets a little bigger, and it even touches his eyes. "Thanks for thinking of it, Jess."

"Of course, Ryan."

"And the best part about it is there can't possibly be anyone to set me up with in the middle of nowhere Vermont, right?"

Jesse's laugh comes out stilted, but Ryan doesn't seem to notice. "Right."

THREE

RYAN ONLY REALIZES he's been asleep when the rental SUV comes to a stop. The stereo's on low—Emmylou Harris—and he's uncomfortably warm in his hoodie, but he knows it's much colder outside. Or is it? He peers out the windshield. They're parked in front of large building with a log facade. He'd expected to see drifts of snow outside, but the ground is bare.

He pulls his spine up straight, glances over at Jesse, who's checking his phone. He'd feel bad about making Jesse drive the whole way except he knows how much Jesse likes to drive. He's a better night driver than Ryan, too. It sometimes seems that Jesse's better at everything than Ryan. Better at dealing with the stress of touring. Better at interacting with their fans. Better at making friends.

Better at life, in general.

Ryan has no idea where he'd be if he hadn't met Jesse, if Jesse hadn't looked at him with those big gray eyes that day in the hospital and made him promise. He hadn't known at the time that promising Jesse he'd look at his songs would lead to the past six years of collaboration. That single day changed the course of his life forever. Some days, Ryan can't even remember life before Jesse. Other days, he remembers, and his blood runs cold at the possibility of never meeting Jesse, of being too stubborn to let him into his life.

Life before Jesse had been all right. Ryan had managed. Life after Jesse was like someone had come into a dark, quiet room and flipped a switch, flooding Ryan's world with color and sound. It hasn't always been easy, but it's miles better than any other option on the table, for Ryan anyway.

It didn't start out that way. At first, Ryan thought he was just being used by an ambitious wannabe singer. Then he realized Jesse had talent and while his nice-guy routine wasn't an act, he was smart enough to know you don't get anywhere in the music industry if you don't exploit your breaks. And Ryan was his break.

But somewhere along the way, it stopped being about debts owed and promises made. Jesse had been right, right from the beginning, back in the hospital when he said they'd be good together. He and Ryan complement each other. Jesse's lyrics are catchy and universal, his melodies haunting and fun in turn. The quality of Ryan's voice makes the lyrics more sophisticated; his bridges turn Jesse's melodies into unforgettable songs. *Hit* songs.

He got used to Jesse, his big smile, his generous spirit, the way he holds a guitar like it's an extension of his body. He's grown to appreciate the way Jesse looks out for him. A first it felt strange to have someone ask if he'd eaten lunch, who pressed water bottles into his hand just when he was starting to feel thirsty, but Jesse simply took it upon himself to take care of him.

Ryan doesn't hate it.

Life isn't all about music for them, either. They've gotten to know each other's families, their friends. Jesse took his first big check from the record company and put a down payment on a house less than a mile from Ryan's on the outskirts of Nashville. Sometimes they go for a week without seeing each other, but rarely a day goes by they don't at least text. Jesse has slowly and surely become the most important person in Ryan's life.

Jesse's a fantastic creative collaborator. He's a level-headed business partner but he's not afraid to think big. He's Ryan's best friend. He wishes he could be content with their work partnership and solid friendship alone. But as the years go by, it's harder and harder to pretend to himself that this is all he wants.

This last year, it's been impossible to deny that Ryan has fallen in love.

Loving Jesse is far too easy. Hell, half the people who meet him are in love with him inside of a minute. Ryan can't even blame them—Jesse's the whole package. Smart, kind, good looking as hell. He gets Ryan, too, knows when to push, when to give him space. No one in Ryan's life has ever put Ryan first the way Jesse does. Of course Ryan loves Jesse.

But he's in love with him, too. The true-blue kind of love the greats sing about, the kind he imagined he might write a song about someday, the kind he'd begun to doubt he'd ever experience for himself. Until he met Jesse.

Not that he fell right away. That kind of enduring love doesn't hit you like a freight train in an instant, it builds and builds over countless days together, over a thousand shared jokes and a million smiles.

Jesse had smiled at him one day—Ryan couldn't say which day exactly, because it was a day like a hundred before it. Jesse had smiled slow and easy like warm molasses, and Ryan had wanted to straddle his hips and lick his mouth to see if he tasted as sweet as his smile. He wanted to kiss him until their lips were chapped and they were breathing each other's air. Somehow his friendly love for Jesse had merged with attraction with devastating results.

Ever since, he's been painfully aware of all of the things he wants from Jesse—not just physical wants, though those are legion, but he has a bone-deep desire for the kind of intimacy they *almost* have together. It would be easy to delude himself that all of their casual touches and shared confidences on the road, in the recording studio, even shooting hoops in Jesse's driveway, mean the same thing to both of them.

Ryan's love for Jesse must be as obvious as a hot pink neon sign over his head. It's too big of a love to keep from shining out of him. When you love someone as much as Ryan loves Jesse, it's hard to hold it in.

But Jesse doesn't know, or he wouldn't be trying to set Ryan up with every available guy in the lower forty-eight. If he knows, that would just be cruel, and Jesse's anything but cruel.

Jesse wants Ryan to be happy, and he thinks that means Ryan should be in a relationship. The more he tries to orchestrate Ryan's next great romance, the more depressed Ryan gets. Because it's hideously obvious that Jesse's never going to feel the way Ryan does. And that makes him wonder if the rest of it— the touring, and the albums, and the projects they've talked about—isn't going to keep working.

How long can Ryan pine away for his best friend before something gives—either Ryan's resolve never to tell him, or his heart breaks one too many times to heal?

He wrote a song about it. Hell, he's written a dozen. Jesse never seems to get that the unattainable love in the songs is *him*. He's a smart guy, but in this one area he has a huge blind spot.

Ryan's not sure if he's happy about that or not. Maybe it would be easier if Jesse knew, if it was all out in the open. Then they could acknowledge it, Jesse could give him a consolatory hug, and they could move on. At least that way maybe Jesse would stop trying to hook him up. Or perhaps he would double his efforts out of guilt. Fuck. No, Ryan's just going to have to keep his feelings to himself. Jesse will just go on being maddening, perfect Jesse. Ryan will go on loving him. Because not loving Jesse, well, that's unthinkable.

At least he's lived with it long enough to know how to act like it never once crossed his mind to find out how Jesse tastes.

From the cozy warmth of the passenger seat, he watches Jesse out of the corner of his eye, wondering if he should let him know he's awake. Maybe he's been waiting on Ryan before going into the lodge.

When Jesse scowls at his phone and taps at the screen impatiently, Ryan says, "Something wrong?"

Jesse looks up at Ryan's voice, turns off his screen abruptly. "You're awake."

Ryan's vaguely aware that Jesse hasn't answered his question but if something is seriously wrong, he'll tell him. "Yeah, I'm awake."

Their gazes lock for a second and Ryan's heart speeds up. There are shadows under Jesse's eyes. He wants to smooth the delicate skin there with his thumb, to bundle him up and bully him into bed the way he knows Jesse's going to do for him in a few minutes. Ryan would gladly take care of Jesse the way Jesse takes care of him. But that's not what they do. Ryan's grumpy, because it's expected, and Jesse's cheerful, even when he doesn't want to be. They fill very specific roles and Ryan doesn't know what would happen if he upset the balance.

Would Jesse let him touch him gently, let him wrap him up in his arms?

Of course not. The idea is painfully ludicrous.

Ryan turns away, opens the door. There may not be snow outside, but it's plenty cold. He shoves his hands in his pockets, finds a knit beanie there and puts it on his head before Jesse can tell him to.

They enter the lodge through big double doors. It's smaller inside than Ryan expected. A narrow entryway leads to a welcome desk, unmanned at this hour.

"They said they'd leave us the keys if no one was

around," Jesse says, striding forward to the desk. He holds up two key rings. "Now we just have to figure out where the cabins are."

"You must be my late arrivals." A voice sounds from the hallway to the right and a second later, a tall, handsome woman with short dark hair walks up to the desk. "Jesse Arlyn?"

"That's right," Jesse says.

"Nice to meet you. I'm Emma. Find the place okay?"

"Easy as pie." He grins at Emma and Ryan douses the flare of jealousy at the twinkle in his eye by reminding himself that Jesse smiles at everyone like that.

"I'll give you a map of the property. You can drive right up to your cabin." She grabs a piece of paper from under the desk and makes a circle on it with a pen. "Number 14. You should find everything you need, but feel free to call down to the desk if there's anything missing."

"Thanks. Breakfast is in this building?" Jesse asks.

"In the restaurant from seven to ten," Emma confirms. "Don't miss the biscuits. They're my family's recipe."

"You own this lodge?" Ryan asks. "We thought there would be snow."

Emma makes a face. "We haven't had snow since Thanksgiving, and that was only an inch. Climate change is real, folks. My grandfather built this place in the fifties. We run it now, me and my brother. Here he is now. Hank, come meet some guests."

A tall, broad-shouldered man emerges from the same hallway Emma appeared from earlier. It takes Ryan a few second to place the familiar face. He's a little grayer than he was six years ago, but his warm brown eyes and salt and pepper beard transport Ryan back to Malawi in an instant.

"Dr. Moore!"

Dr. Hank Moore's face breaks into a wide smile. "Ryan Winslow? It's been a while, hasn't it? How the hell have you been?"

Ryan senses Jesse stepping up to his side, and he turns to share his astonishment. Jesse looks just as surprised to see the man who worked in the field hospital in Malawi and treated his injured arm, but no less pleased than Ryan.

"Dr. Moore, hi!"

Dr. Moore's gaze shifts and his smile gets bigger, if possible. "Jesse Arlyn, too. Wow, this is wild. And call me Hank, please."

"What are you doing here?" Ryan asks.

"I work here, live here. Left the Corps about four years ago, came back to my hometown to figure out what I wanted to do next and never left. Luckily, the town doctor was ready for retirement, so I took over for her about three years ago. But what about you two—I hear your names once in a while. Rock stars or something aren't you?"

"Humble country musicians, Doc," Jesse says, showing his dimple slyly.

Ryan snorts. "This humble country musician got a Grammy nomination last year," he says, pointing a finger at Jesse.

Dr. Moore—Hank—whistles. "I always had a feeling

you'd be on to great things."

"Couldn't have done it without Ryan," Jesse says.

The fondness in his eyes activates the stupid, useless part of Ryan's heart that wants to hope.

"We're coming off a tour, actually," Ryan says. "We're staying here for a week to work on our new Christmas album."

Jesse's look of fondness turns to one of astonishment, perhaps at how enthusiastic Ryan sounds about the Christmas album. He's still not sure it's not going to be massively corny, but he did agree to give it a try.

"Well, I hope I'll get to see something of you while you're here," Hank says. He glances between the two of them. "You're not only here to work, right? Maybe we could grab dinner tomorrow night."

"Definitely," Jesse says.

"Wait, what cabin are you in? Emma, did you give them 12?"

"14," she answers.

"Oh no, if 12 is free, you have to take it. There's a skylight over the bed, and a sunken hot tub. Perfect for a couple's getaway."

Jesse seems to realize what Hank's implying first, because he laughs while Ryan's still processing. "Oh, no, we're not a couple, though the hot tub sounds amazing. We're just friends, despite what some fans believe." He laughs again and the sound grates on Ryan's ears.

"Yeah," he echoes weakly, "just friends."

"Oh." Hank doesn't seem fazed, but his gaze narrows slightly on Ryan. "Okay. Well, then 14 works. It's got two awesome bedrooms. No hot tub, but it does have a huge soaking tub. Let me or Emma know if you need anything."

"I already told them that," Emma says. "Now let them settle in, Hank. It's late. You can shoot the shit about your days in the Corps tomorrow."

Hank rolls his eyes and Ryan misses his own sister for a single, fierce second. "Fair enough. It's really nice to see you two. Let me give you my cell number."

"Ryan, can you grab it?" Jesse says quickly.

Ryan takes out his phone and texts the number Hank recites to him so Hank has his number, too, then they all say goodbye with promises to get together tomorrow.

Jesse has the map and the keys, and they hustle out to the SUV which has gone cold in the intervening minutes. "What a small world," he says, starting the car up and heading down the narrow track behind the main lodge building.

"You had no idea this was Hank Moore's place?" Ryan asks. He yawns, suddenly exhausted despite his nap.

"I swear, I had no idea," Jesse says with such vehemence that Ryan's antennae perk up. Why would Jesse be so defensive? Unless he thinks Ryan thinks that he knew Hank would be here. And the only reason that would bother Ryan is if he....

"You aren't trying to set me up with Dr. Moore, are you?" he asks, stomach tightening nervously.

Jesse pulls the SUV to a stop at a large wood frame cabin with the number 14 carved into a post at the front. He shifts in his seat, looks Ryan directly in the eyes and says, "I had no idea he'd be here, I swear, Ryan."

Ryan believes him. Jesse's not a liar. Even still, his neck itches as if he's forgotten something as they carry their bags into the well-appointed, spacious cabin. He gives up trying to put his finger on the sensation and chalks it up to disappointment at hearing Jesse laugh at the idea they could be a couple. It's not like Ryan doesn't know his feelings are unrequited, but it still hurts to hear it straight from Jesse how laughable the idea of them being together actually is.

He takes a modicum of satisfaction in putting dibs on the slightly bigger bedroom. He's got to take his wins where he can get them. Still, it takes a long time to fall asleep that night, listening to Jesse get ready for bed in the room next door.

FOUR

JESSE'S not exactly a morning person, but Ryan *really* isn't a morning person. He's still snoozing when Jesse throws on a jacket and boots and grabs his key before quietly closing the front door of their cabin and heading to the main lodge for breakfast. And reconnaissance.

He wasn't lying to Ryan when he said he had no idea Hank Moore would be here. He hasn't lied to Ryan about anything. They really do need to work on the album, and this place is perfect for that, even though, disappointingly, there's no snow. The only thing he didn't tell Ryan was the reason he picked Pine Tree Lodge was that Cameron, Ryan's ex, is supposed to be here, too.

Cameron just finished up a stint as the keyboardist for a big pop act touring Asia. When Jesse heard through mutual friends Cameron was heading back to the States, he got in touch. Cameron's from Columbia, Vermont, originally, and he told Jesse he planned to stay here through the holidays. When Jesse looked the place up and saw how great it would be for a work retreat, he hatched a plan.

Ryan and Cameron broke up about a year ago, and Jesse is pretty sure it wasn't a coincidence that soon after Ryan's songs started getting wistful and sad. They seem to constantly reference a love who is forever out of reach. Clearly, he still has feelings for Cameron. If Jesse can't get him to go out with any of the eligible guys he finds, well, then he can put him back in the path of his ex. He told Cameron they would both come up to Vermont for a week, but he didn't tell Ryan because he wasn't sure Ryan wouldn't duck out. And if something went wrong, he didn't want to get Ryan's hopes up.

He's glad he listened to that instinct, because as soon as they arrived last night and Jesse checked his messages, he'd learned Cameron had been delayed and might not be there for a few more days. What the hell? If he was the one who hadn't seen Ryan in a year, nothing would stop him from being here.

Okay, so Cameron isn't around. That doesn't mean the time will be wasted. It's going to be awesome to see Hank and catch up. And if the flare of interest he saw in Hank's eyes last night when he learned Ryan and Jesse were just friends wasn't just a trick of the light, it won't hurt to see if Hank might be an alternative to Cameron. A year apart might have changed the way Ryan and Cameron feel about each other. Jesse is pretty sure Dr. Moore is bi, like him. They kept stuff like that on the down low in the Corps, not because their coworkers cared, but because sometimes the areas where they worked had anti-gay laws and no one wanted to get tangled up in red tape in their host countries.

He finds the main room of the lodge easily by following the delicious breakfast smells, including coffee. The mild weather doesn't look like it has affected bookings. There are half a dozen tables filled with hungry guests, and a roaring fire in the circular fire pit at the center of the room. The place has been decorated for the Christmas season, with a large silver-and-gold decorated tree in the corner, and pretty swaths of greenery tied with red bows on all the dark wood-paneled walls. The place feels homey and yet a bit grand. Jesse settles into an empty table near the fire pit and sighs happily. He's actually looking forward to relaxing while he's here. He's worn out from the tour and the late night of driving.

"Good morning. Coffee?" A young woman appears next to his table holding out a silver carafe.

Jesse turns his coffee cup up gratefully. "Please."

"Pretty much everyone gets the Lodge Special, but if you want something else, I can see what I can do."

"Does the Lodge Special come with biscuits?"

The woman, petite with dark hair and eyes, smiles. "You know it."

"Sold."

The server bustles away and while he waits for his breakfast, stomach rumbling, he checks his phone. This close to the holidays, things are slowing down on the work front, thank god. He knows Sadie, his and Ryan's manager, and Hector, their tour manager, can handle most anything that might come up. He needs to buy Christmas presents for his family, though, and confirm his and Ryan's flight to home to Nashville next week. Though if Cameron actually shows up, he and Ryan might decide to spend the holidays together. It'll kind of suck to fly back to Tennessee alone, but if Ryan's smile reaches his eyes again, it'll be worth it.

He looks up from texting his mom to ask for gift ideas for his dad when the server comes back with a plate laden with food.

"This looks amazing, thank you."

She sets down jars of peach jam and marmalade, clearly homemade. "I thought you might enjoy both."

"You thought right. Hey, what's your name?"

"Joy," she says, her smile turning more personal. "What's yours?"

"Jesse," he says, sparing a dimple for her. She's cute, but that's not why he's asking. "You know Hank Moore, Joy?"

Her eyebrows knit together. "Sure, everyone knows Dr. Moore. He's my boss's brother."

"Maybe this is a weird question, but is he married, or seeing anyone, as far as you know?"

The groove between Joy's eyebrows intensifies. "Excuse me?"

Jesse winces at her understandable wariness over the personal question and hurries to explain. "We were in the Peace Corps together, and I haven't seen him in years. Just wondering what he's been up to."

She relaxes slightly. "He's single, I think. I heard he was dating a teacher at the high school for a little while, but that was last year."

"A teacher?"

"Yeah, Mr. Hodge. He teaches biology." Joy frowns, as if she's regretting telling him, but Jesse turns on his most charming smile.

"Thanks, Joy. I can't wait to try these biscuits."

"So, what about you?" she asks, her good mood restored. "You were in the Peace Corps? That's so cool."

Jesse laughs a little. "It was cool," he says. "I learned a lot."

"Maybe you could tell me more about it. I cover the desk in the afternoons."

"Yeah, maybe." The last leg of tour was so busy, and he's been so preoccupied with Ryan that Jesse hasn't been with anyone in a while. Joy is attractive and seems interested, but ending his own dry spell isn't a priority.

She shrugs off his lukewarm response and tops up his coffee before she goes to wait on another table.

Jesse digs into his breakfast, checking his phone one more time. No word from Cameron. His mom texted back though, suggesting a home brewing kit for his dad, who recently retired and has been having a hard time filling his days. He files that idea away, then puts his phone in his pocket. He doesn't want to be one of those people who has to be on his phone when he's alone. Instead, he slathers marmalade on one half of the biscuit and peach jam on the other, and gazes around the room. Two women share a table not far away. Their ankles touch under the table and one's talking animatedly while the other looks on with a fond tilt of her head.

Jesse's chest aches all of a sudden. The quiet one's expression seems so familiar, somehow. He thinks they must be really close friends for half a second, until his heteronormativity goggles fall away, and he realizes they're a couple. Something about them makes him feel kind of—sad? Which doesn't make any sense, because they seem perfectly happy, and young love is always something to celebrate.

Young love. Hmmm. He opens his phone up again to jot down a couple of words in his notes app. Maybe there's a song there.

When he looks up from his phone, the women are standing up to leave. He watches them go, walking so close their arms brush, still inexplicably unsettled. He must just be tired.

Joy stops by to check on him again, and he orders a Lodge Special to take back to Ryan. A few minutes later, she brings him a large paper bag and a steaming paper cup of coffee. He juggles both carefully as he passes by the main desk, hoping to run into Hank or Emma, but there's someone new there, an older man with short gray hair, who smiles at him pleasantly. Jesse nods back, then walks up the road to the cabins. In the light of day, he can see just how well situated the property is, the Green Mountains a backdrop for the evergreen woods behind the buildings. It really would be beautiful with snow, but it's nice that it's not so cold that he doesn't even need gloves.

When he gets to cabin 14, he struggles with the key and the food for a minute, then wises up and puts the bag down on the wooden step. He's got the key in the lock when the door opens unexpectedly, Ryan on the other side.

His friend looks like he just woke up, his light brown

hair all mashed on one side, his cheeks covered in more than one day of stubble. He's wearing a long-sleeved gray T-shirt and tattered plaid pants Jesse's pretty sure he's owned since the Peace Corps days. He's just staring at Jesse and Jesse realizes he's staring back.

"So are you coming in or what?" Ryan's voice is sleep rough.

Jesse swallows. It's not like he doesn't know Ryan's attractive. He's had a first-row seat to Ryan's attractiveness for six years. But he doesn't think about it all the time. How could he—he'd never get anything done if all he thought about was the way Ryan's shoulders fill out his always slightly-too-small shirts and the way his pretty pink tongue sticks out of his mouth a little bit when he's concentrating real hard. So it takes him by surprise sometimes, when he looks at Ryan and really sees him.

How is anyone who looks like Ryan still single?

"I brought breakfast," he says belatedly. "And coffee." He hands Ryan the cup and reaches down for the bag.

"Coffee. I love you," Ryan says. He's inhaling steam from the cup, so Jesse's pretty sure he's declaring his love for the coffee, not Jesse, but there's still something about the phrase that makes Jesse's stomach jump.

"You'll love the biscuits, too," Jesse says, trying to shake off the weird mood he's been in all morning. He shuts the door behind them, follows Ryan to the little kitchenette in the corner of the main room. He finds a plate and a set of cutlery in a cabinet and unpacks the food.

"You ate?" Ryan asks, after he's drunk about half the coffee in one go.

"Yeah. Stuffed. You gotta try this marmalade." He takes the plate to the coffee table. "And maybe later we can go for a walk or something. It's a beautiful day. Not cold at all."

Ryan's bottom lip pops out in a pout. "You said there'd be snow."

Jesse looks away from Ryan's mouth. "Yeah. I know. I'll see what I can do, okay?"

He can't help seeing Ryan's lips curve into a smile out of the corner of his eye. "Yeah, you do that, Jess."

Jesse chokes out a laugh, feeling odd in his skin. What the hell is going on with him? He's about to steal a piece of Ryan's bacon when there's a chiming noise. Ryan's phone.

Ryan pulls it out of his pocket, reads the message. "It's Hank. He wants to do dinner with us later."

Right, Hank. And Cameron. And the album. There are way more important things going on than whatever Jesse's stupid stomach is doing whenever Ryan's attention is on him. They're here to make Ryan happy. That's all that matters to Jesse.

"Awesome. Tell him we're in."

FIVE

"SO HE'S COOKING for us? We should bring something, like a bottle of wine," Ryan calls through the open door of his bedroom as they're getting ready to head to Hank's for an early dinner. Apparently, Dr. Moore lives in the main lodge building and has his own kitchen. Ryan hopes he's a good cook because they skipped lunch and he's starving.

"We're fresh out of wine, but I do have some bourbon," Jesse says a moment later, appearing at the door holding a bottle of dark amber liquid. "Brought it for us, but I guess we can always get more."

"Good call." This is what Ryan means when he says Jesse's better at everything than him. Of course he'd have the perfect host gift just lying around, while Ryan's having trouble picking a shirt to wear.

"Wear the green one," Jesse says, pointing to the shirt Ryan had already considered and discarded on the bed. Before Ryan can argue, he disappears. He's almost about to wear the brown one out of spite, but Jesse's probably right. Green's more festive for Christmas, anyway. He buttons up the shirt, tucks it into his best pair of jeans. Cowboy boots, hair combed, and he's ready for a nice night out. Most of the time he dresses down, but he enjoys polishing up once in a while. If they were in Tennessee, he'd probably don his cowboy hat, but that seems like overkill for Vermont.

Jesse's dressed similarly in jeans, boots, and a dark blue button down made fancier by a bit of white stitching. He's recently shaved, and Ryan can't help but notice how good he smells, even from across the room.

By unspoken agreement they hadn't done any work today, just lazed around the cabin, then went for a walk around the property and into the foothills behind the lodge. The fresh air and exercise felt good, and it was a relief not to have to think about the next stop on the tour, gearing up the mental and emotional energy for live performing. Jesse had been quiet, for him at least. When they got back to the cabin, he'd gone to take a nap before dinner, while Ryan called his mom and his sister to catch up.

"Got your coat?" Jesse asks before they leave the cabin. Ryan's about to protest that he doesn't need it, but now that the sun's down there's plenty of chill in the air and he grabs it. Jesse has the bourbon and together they walk down the road to the lodge.

"So, how do you want to do this?" Ryan asks.

"Huh?" Jesse looks as if he's been miles away.

"The Christmas album. I know we have to do some covers, but we have to decide which ones, and we'll have at least a few original songs. What do you want to work on first?" Ryan hadn't exactly wanted to do a Christmas album, but he does have to admit their fans would love it, and it would be one less album he owes the studio on his contract. He and Jesse have never put out a joint album before, either. If it goes well, maybe they'll do another one of all originals.

"Oh, right. Well, we could start with the covers, figure out the mood, and then fill in with some of our own. You got anything Christmassy I haven't heard?"

Ryan's about to give him a hard no, but he reconsiders. He's got a ballad he worked on last winter and never finished. He could tweak it, give it a holiday gloss. "Maybe. You?"

"Just bits and pieces. I'll drag them out for you tomorrow."

"Sounds good." He's glad when they reach the main building. His nose feels cold and he's sure it's as red as Rudolph's.

Emma's at the desk. "Hi there," she says warmly. "Hank asked me to walk you back to his place."

They fall into step behind her as she takes them down a hallway lined with black and white photographs that showcase the lodge through the years.

"It's so cool that you're carrying on your grandparents' legacy," Ryan says.

"Hank and I practically grew up here and I could never imagine living anyplace else. But Hank wanted to see the world." Emma points at one of the photos. Ryan leans in and sees two little dark-haired kids next to a man and a woman with eighties-style haircuts. "Our parents weren't in love with this place like I was, so when I showed interest in taking over the place, they were only too happy to sign it over to me and take early retirement. They live in Florida now. I thought Hank would never come home, but it's been really nice since he did. He's still helping people in town, and I don't feel quite so alone rattling around this place."

Ryan wonders why she's still single. She's attractive, and clearly the lodge is doing well. Columbia's small, and the next big city is an hour away, so maybe she just has trouble meeting people. Then he stops himself. Her love life is none of his business. Jesse's persistent match-making must be infecting his brain. He shakes his head and follows Emma down another corridor where she stops in front of a door and knocks before letting herself in.

Ryan realizes he was expecting a glorified hotel room, but Hank's place is more like the inside of a regular house, with a cozy living room complete with Christmas tree and a big country-style kitchen attached, where they find Hank, who accepts the bottle of bourbon with a grin. Emma chats with them for a minute before excusing herself to go back to work.

"Saul will take the desk for you if you want to stay," Hank says, but Emma laughs.

"I don't want to get in the way of all the manly remi-niscing you're going to do," she says. "But Jesse, Ryan, I'm sure I'll see you around."

Emma leaves, and Ryan shrugs off his coat, laying it on the back of a straight-backed kitchen chair. The kitchen reminds him a little of his grandmother's.

"Tell me you're hungry, because I took the roast

chicken out of the oven fifteen minutes ago. Just about to carve it up," Hank says.

"Starving," Ryan says. "We skipped lunch."

"Too full from the lodge breakfast," Jesse adds. "What can we do to help?"

Hank gives Jesse a bottle of wine and a corkscrew, and hands Ryan a wooden salad bowl filled with a green salad. "Can you take these out to the table?"

He nods to another door off the kitchen and Ryan realizes there's a separate dining room. The long wooden table is already laid with three places. He puts the salad bowl in the center of the table next to a bowl of mashed potatoes and looks around.

"This place is gorgeous." It feels old fashioned, but in the best way, homey and real.

Jesse hums in apparent agreement, struggling with the wine bottle for a minute before Ryan smiles and takes it from him. It only takes him a second to get the cork out with a satisfying pop. Maybe he's better at one thing than his friend.

Hank comes in a second later carrying the roast chicken, fragrant and mouthwatering with crispy brown skin.

"This place is attached to the lodge, but it feels like an old farmhouse," Ryan remarks as they go about the business of serving themselves food and wine.

"You're right on the money," Hank says, putting a slice of chicken on Ryan's plate. "This was the original house back when this was a dairy farm. When my grandparents bought the property in the fifties, they soon realized dairy farming was not for them, so they sold the livestock and razed the barns for cabins, then added onto this original building in fits and starts until it got to be this big sprawling thing. My parents modernized everything in the eighties and nineties and now Emma's working on making everything energy efficient and green. She's got an apartment in the other wing, but I like this part of the place. Though it's a little too big for just me, when I'm at the clinic five days a week."

"Would be a great place for kids," Jesse says, with a glance at Ryan. "We saw the picture of you and Emma in the hallway."

Hank laughs. "She and I are doing a terrible job of making the next generation to take over this place. But who knows what'll happen in the future."

"Yeah, so you aren't seeing anyone?" Jesse asks.

Ryan shoots him a look, but Jesse pointedly keeps his gaze on Hank.

He doesn't seem bothered by the question. "No. Things have been busy at work. We're trying to raise money to extend the clinic's hours. Now if something happens during our off hours you either have to take your chances calling 911, but response times can be long depending on where you live, or get someone to drive you to the hospital forty-five minutes away. When I first got here, I told people they could call me day or night, but I realized that was unsustainable."

Ryan's not surprised that Hank's trying to help as many people as possible. "What do you mean, raise money? Who runs the clinic?"

"It's funded by the town, actually. We're too small to be of any interest to the big corporate healthcare companies. I've been trying to put together a fundraiser for the new year."

Ryan frowns. Hank shouldn't have to raise money on top of the work of doctoring people. It reminds him that while they helped a lot of people in the Peace Corps, there are still plenty of needs right here at home.

"Well, let us know if we can help," Jesse says, taking the words out of Ryan's mouth. "And by the way, this is the best roast chicken I've had since my mama's."

"High praise," Hank says. He looks at them and smiles, his eyes crinkling. "It's really good to see you boys. Now, tell me everything that happened since you left Malawi. How's your arm, Jesse?"

Jesse rubs the back of his right arm with his left hand in a gesture Ryan's seen him do a thousand times. It never fails to make him a little dizzy, remembering that day, the worry that Jesse was going to bleed out before they got back to the camp.

He blinks and remembers they're safe and warm and in Vermont of all places. Jesse's telling Hank about the first song they collaborated on, that it became a hit single off Ryan's quote-unquote-comeback album about a year after they got back from the Corps. How that led to more and more chances to work together, Jesse's solo album, Ryan's last album which was half made up of their collaborations, and three live tours, the most recent of which spit them out in Boston and now Pine Tree Lodge.

"We're working on a Christmas album. It'll come out next year, of course, but I thought it would be better if we could get into it while it's actually Christmastime,"

Jesse says, smiling at Ryan. "Some of us have more Christmas spirit than others."

"Hey, I like Christmas," Ryan protests. "I just don't like Christmas *albums*. They're so hokey and trite and corny."

"I know, I know," Jesse says. "But I already told you, ours won't be. I promise."

"Just like you promised me snow?" Ryan takes a sip of wine. He's enjoying needling Jesse. It takes his mind off that fact that when they go back to their shared cabin, instead of crawling into Jesse's warm bed and warming the sheets together, he'll be tossing and turning in a cold bed alone.

Jesse groans. "Hank, what are the chances of it snowing while we're here?"

Hank shrugs. "I honestly don't know. We often have a white Christmas, but that's a couple of weeks away yet. Thankfully, we're not a ski lodge, though we do have cross country trails nearby, and snowshoes available if people want to tramp through the woods. I think if you want snow, you'll have to go farther north. Winter's been unpredictable lately."

"Bein' a simple Tennessee boy, I always assumed Vermont had snow from Thanksgiving to Easter," Jesse says, laying his accent on thick.

Ryan snorts a laugh. "You're an idiot," he says, and he worries he's let too much affection slip into his words when Jesse's eyes narrow on him almost imperceptibly.

"But snow or not, I sure am glad you two picked Pine Tree Lodge for your vacation, or working vacation, it seems. How'd you find out about us, anyway?" Hank asks as they clear the table.

Jesse fumbles his plate and his fork falls to the floor with a clatter. "Uh. Through a friend."

Ryan's surprised. He'd thought maybe Sadie or Hector recommended it. "Which friend?"

"Uh, is that apple pie?" Jesse points to what is obviously an apple pie on the counter in the kitchen. Hank's putting away the leftovers, and he nods.

"Not homemade, sorry. I can't bake to save my life. But there's a really nice little farm stand a few miles down the road. Around the holidays they do pies, fruit-cake, the works. Ryan, can you get the ice cream out of the freezer?"

Ryan groans. "I honestly don't know if can eat another bite after that amazing dinner."

"I can," Jesse says with enthusiasm. "And you can, too. It's practically un-American to pass up apple pie a la mode, Ryan." He rubs the scar on the back of his arm; Ryan wonders if he's even aware he's doing it.

"A little piece won't hurt, I guess."

Jesse beams and Ryan finds himself smiling back, even though inwardly he's cringing. Could he be more pathetic, getting all warm and gooey at making Jesse happy with the simple act of agreeing to dessert?

He sighs. Hank's fingers brush his as he hands him a plate with a small slice of pie and a modest scoop of ice cream. He has long fingers, big hands. Not as big as Jesse's, though. He sighs again as they settle into soft chairs in the snug living room to eat.

Why can't he find Hank attractive? He is, objectively, but it's hard to separate this Hank, who makes a mean roast chicken and whose eyes crinkle when he smiles from Dr. Moore, competent field doctor who sewed Jesse's arm up. He doesn't exactly remember the land mine explosion fondly, and he supposes his feelings about Hank are tangled up with that.

His thoughts are derailed when Jesse moans, the noise bordering the obscene.

"This pie is incredible," Jesse says with his mouth full. Ryan wants to crawl into his lap and lick the crumbs out of his mouth.

And that's the problem in a nutshell. There's no way Hank or any other guy is getting a second glance from Ryan while he feels this stupid over his best friend.

"Try this, Ryan." Jesse points to his plate. The ice cream's starting to melt and Ryan really doesn't have an appetite, but he scoops up a small bite and tastes it. The cinnamon and sugar can't quite cover up the taste of longing.

"It's real good, Jess," Ryan says to appease Jesse's questioning face.

His expression relaxes into a pleased smile. "Hey Hank, maybe if you have some free time this week you could take Ryan to the farm stand."

Hank raises his eyebrows. "I could do that," he says, glancing at Ryan. "If I'm not on shift, I'd be happy to. Just say the word."

Ryan stands up abruptly, feeling a little sick. "Can I use your bathroom?"

Hank directs him through the door at the other end of the living room, putting a hand on the small of his back briefly. Ryan finds the bathroom and splashes cold water on his face, looking at himself in the mirror.

He can't keep doing this to himself, taking every scrap of affection from Jesse and wishing it was more, all while Jesse's pushing him into the path every available guy they meet as if he's a loser who can't get his own date.

He closes his eyes and wracks his brain. There's got to be a solution. He's tried wishing away his feelings. He's tried working them out in his songs. He's tried ignoring Jesse and failed miserably; he can't make it six hours without texting him or responding to one of his texts.

He opens his eyes and glares at his reflection. If Jesse wants him to be in a relationship so much, then maybe he should just do it. Jesse's not vying for the job of his boyfriend, so he might as well force himself to move on. And if Ryan being with someone would make Jesse happy, well, Ryan's maybe just sick enough to want to do it for that reason alone.

He thinks about Hank's eye crinkles and his attractive smile and his beard. He imagines kissing Hank, feeling his beard scrape his chin, tickle his mouth. It's not a repulsive image. Ryan may be in love with someone else, but it's been so long since he's been with someone that the idea of making out with a man as objectively appealing as Hank is kind of working for him.

He takes a deep, measured breath. "You can do this," he says, then he returns to the living room, picks up the bottle of bourbon Jesse brought and pastes on a grin. "You want to crack this sucker open, Hank?"

Hank chuckles. "I can't get too deep into that bottle, but I'd be glad to have a snort."

Jesse claps his hands. "Now we're talking."

"Actually, Jesse—didn't you need to go call your mom?" Ryan lifts his eyebrows meaningfully at him.

"Huh?"

Ryan glances at Hank, then at the door. "Yeah. You said you'd call your mom before it got too late. Don't worry about me, I've got a key to the cabin."

Jesse nods slowly at first, then faster as he picks up what Ryan's putting down. "Right. Yeah, I better go. Thanks for everything, Hank."

"It's been so great to catch up with you, Jesse. Thanks for coming." Hank hugs him and Jesse claps him on the back. He finds his jacket and then he's glancing at Ryan.

"Well, uh. See you later, Ryan. Don't keep Hank up too late," he says on short laugh.

And then he's gone and it's just Ryan and Hank in the cozy living room.

Ryan screws up his courage. "Now, how about that bourbon?"

SIX

JESSE LETS himself into the cabin and fumbles to turn on a lamp. The place feels empty and cold, even though it's probably thirty degrees warmer than the outside air. He hadn't exactly planned on coming home alone, and now he doesn't know what to do with himself. He's too keyed up to go to sleep. He glances at his phone. He supposes he could actually call his mama.

Why is he so out of sorts, anyway? The evening had gone well, and if Ryan sometimes seemed withdrawn, that was just Ryan lately. But then it was like a switch had flipped and all of a sudden Ryan had practically shoved him out the door.

Good. Right? Ryan's an adult, and if he wants one-on-one time with Hank, then who is Jesse to get in the way?

He sighs and kicks off his boots. The thing is, it's not just Ryan and Hank catching up on old times. It's Ryan and Hank and a bottle of bourbon. That implies they'll be drinking. Ryan gets looser when he drinks. Less inhibited. Touchy-feely, too.

Jesse wrenches open the buttons on his shirt, cussing when one pops off and skitters across the floor. But why should he care? This is what he's been hoping for, what he's been, okay, yes, scheming, to make happen for weeks. Months, really. Ever since the intermittent sadness in Ryan's eyes became more of a permanent feature.

So why does the thought of Ryan and Hank sharing a bottle of the good stuff make his stomach hurt? Maybe he really is sick? Except he was fine at dinner. Ryan's eyes had been bluer than blue tonight, set off nicely by the shirt Jesse suggested he wear. It had been great to reconnect with Hank, and the meal was delicious.

No, he's not getting sick. He's just...worried about Ryan. Yeah. That's it. Ryan seemed a little out of sorts when they were having dessert and then all of a sudden he made a move on Hank and the whole thing seems out of character.

Except, is it? Ryan tends to go for guys he knows and trusts instead of one-night stands with strangers. He must feel comfortable with Hank, comfortable enough to let his guard down and drink with the man. And maybe more.

Jesse's suddenly assaulted by the intrusive mental picture of Ryan and Hank, drinking and laughing and talking. Kissing. He can't seem to stop picturing the two of them together and it's weird. He's never imagined Ryan's hookups before. But this time, it's all he can think about.

He finishes undressing, not bothering to look for his lost button, puts on sleep clothes. He's not tired, but he doesn't want to hang out in the common area of the cabin as if he's waiting up for Ryan or anything. That's ridiculous. He leaves a light burning for him, though, and then climbs into bed with his phone and finds a mindless comedy to watch. He starts yawning halfway through and even though Ryan's not home yet, he forces himself to be a grownup, turns off his phone, and closes his eyes.

HE FEELS like he's only been asleep for a few minutes, but the bedside clock shows it's after midnight when he wakes to a shuffling noise outside his door. He listens for a minute, his heart racing. The sounds resolve themselves into someone trying to be quiet and failing. Ryan must be back.

Jesse shuts his eyes again, debating whether to go out there or not. He kind of wants to make sure Ryan's okay, but he has no reason to think he wouldn't be. Besides, there's something hot and twisting in his gut that doesn't want to see Ryan if he's just hooked up with Hank.

The noises stop anyway, and Jesse slowly relaxes back into bed. He'll see Ryan in the morning and if anything happened with Hank, Ryan can tell him then.

He tries to go back to sleep but he's still wide-awake minutes later with the aftereffects of adrenaline running through him. He's thirsty, too. Quietly, he slips out of bed and opens the door to the common area. The light he'd left for Ryan is still burning. It's useful to have it to see by as he walks through the living room to the kitchenette, fills a glass with tap water, and heads back to his room. The door to Ryan's room is ajar, and he pauses when he hears a noise from within. Maybe he should just go check on Ryan for a second. He takes a step toward Ryan's door, and hears the noise again, louder.

It's a moan.

Jesse cocks his head. A moan of pain? But then he hears another noise, the sound of rustling sheets, and what sounds like the slide of skin on skin.

Fuck. Ryan's jerking off.

In the six years they've known each other they've shared close quarters from time to time. Touring together puts them in each other's personal space plenty. But they always have their own rooms on the road, and Ryan's a naturally private guy. Jesse, to his knowledge, has never, ever had so much of a hint that Ryan even masturbated at all, much less heard him do it. And he's definitely never seen Ryan more naked than wearing swimming trunks at a pool.

But now he's hovering a couple of feet outside of Ryan's door, listening to his best friend get himself off and it's doing things to him that he can't explain. He wants to run away. He wants to open the door and watch. He wants—he wants not to have the mental image of Ryan touching himself in the next room while he tries to fall asleep.

And he very much wishes he could rethink his late-night sojourn to get water when he hears Ryan's voice formulate a sound. "Ahhh."

Oh fuck. Was that Ryan coming? Was he—was he coming thinking about Hank?

Jesse doesn't wait for Ryan to come down from his orgasm, just walks as quietly and as quickly as he can back to his room, where he shuts his door soundlessly and gets back into bed. He sets the water on the night table, puts a pillow over his head and wills himself to go to sleep.

It's almost dawn before he finally succumbs.

SEVEN

RYAN'S not as hungover as he thought he might be when he rolls over and opens his eyes to sunlight coming through his window. He forgot to put the shades all the way down last night and even though it's much earlier than he usually likes to be up, he has warring needs to take a piss and drink a gallon of water, so he shoves out of bed and stumbles to the bathroom. He takes care of business and then fills a water bottle and chugs half of it. The shower wakes him up enough to relive last night's debacle in excruciating detail.

The first part hadn't been so bad. Then Jesse left and it was just him and Hank. Again, not the end of the world. Hank's easy on the eyes, easy to talk to. Easy, period. And he's interested, or Ryan thinks he is. Maybe he's written Ryan off after he'd stalled, drunk a couple more fingers of bourbon than he should have had, then planted a sloppy kiss on Hank's mouth.

Hank, decent human being that he is, had gently pushed Ryan away, saying something about not wanting to do this when Ryan was drunk. Ryan's face heats just thinking about it. He can't even get a casual hookup right. But he's glad Hank hadn't let things go further. He'd probably feel even shittier.

But he feels like a tease, and while the kiss with Hank—brief as it was—was okay, it just reminded him of what he wants with Jesse. What he wants and what he's never going to have. He stumbled home in the dark and the cold and the minute he'd come in the cabin and smelled Jesse's cologne, his dick had hardened up and he'd had to do something about it before passing out.

He wishes he could say it was the first time he'd fallen asleep directly after jerking off to the fantasy of his best friend sucking his cock.

He gets dressed and drinks some more water. Jesse's bedroom door is closed. Looks like it's Ryan's turn to go out and find breakfast.

THE LODGE great room is warm and cozy and smells amazing. He gets a table by the fire pit in the center of the room, trying to feel the festive spirit. Christmas is just around the corner now. He already had gifts shipped home, and Jesse's in charge of their plane tickets back to Austin when their work-slash-vacation week is up. He's actually looking forward to a quiet holiday.

He's been dosed with coffee from a smiling server who tells him her name is Joy, and orders the Lodge Special for himself, plus one to go.

"Is the one to go for Jesse?" Joy asks, startling him.

"Uh, yeah?"

"I'll make sure they put in extra marmalade. He was practically licking the jar clean yesterday," she says with a twinkle in her eye.

He laughs. "Sounds like Jesse."

"I'll be right back with your breakfast."

Ryan checks his texts and is about to search for a few Christmas songs they might want to cover, even though Jesse probably has a list prepared, when Joy comes back with his food. Only when he looks up from the steaming plate that's been placed in front of him, it's not Joy but Hank smiling down at him.

"Oh, hey," Ryan says weakly, willing himself not to blush.

"Can I join you? I was stealing some coffee from the kitchen, and I saw your order come up."

"Sure."

Hank takes the seat across from Ryan, a silver travel mug in his hands.

Ryan looks at his plate, appetite suddenly gone. He glances at Hank, who seems relaxed. "You aren't eating?"

"Already ate, but I was out of coffee. I have to go check in at the clinic in a minute, but I wanted to come say hi. Make sure you're doing okay."

"Oh, you mean the bourbon."

Hank raises his eyebrows. "You were a little hammered."

"Nah, not that bad. I'm feeling pretty good."

"Well, don't forget to hydrate. Doctor's orders."

Ryan lets himself smile. "I won't. And thanks again for dinner, it was great. Sorry about—"

"Don't be sorry, Ryan. It was fun to catch up." Hank

leans across the table. "Jesse's not with you this morning?"

"Still sleeping."

Hank nods. "You know, if you ever need to talk, I've been told I'm a good listener."

"What would I need to talk about?"

"You didn't have any trouble talking last night about the tour, and your music, and your family, and your views on the Nashville Predators, but there was one big glaring omission in your conversation topics."

Ryan's going to regret asking. "What was that?"

"Jesse Arlyn. Specifically, your feelings about him."

If Ryan's appetite hadn't already fled, it would have disappeared at those words.

"He doesn't know, does he?" Hank says kindly.

"Know what?" Ryan hates himself for asking, but there's a part of him desperate to talk to someone who knows both of them. Could maybe help him get his head back on straight.

"How you feel about him," Hank says patiently. "I get it. Half the girls and a quarter of the guys we worked with in the Corps had crushes on him. He was a little young for me back then, but I saw what they saw. He never seemed aware of it. He just flirted with everyone equally."

"Yeah, well." Ryan knows he's barely better than a groupie, but it stings to hear someone else say it.

Hank frowns. "It's not the same, Ryan. It's none of my business, I know—"

"It sort of became your business when I kissed you,"

Ryan mumbles. Jesus, this is one of the most mortifying conversations of his life.

"Look, you and I don't know each other that well. The Corps was a long time ago, and we were only in Malawi for a few months together. But I worked with Jesse for almost two years. And as smart and as tough and as kind as that kid—well, I guess he's not a kid anymore—as that man is, I do know he has a couple of blind spots. One is that he thinks he's got to earn people's respect by being what he thinks they need, rather than just being himself. For such a smart guy, he's not the most self-aware."

Is that true? Jesse is a bit of a people pleaser, Ryan will admit.

"But he cares about you, and after seeing the two of you together a couple of times, I'm going to offer you a little free advice," Hank says.

Ryan lifts a skeptical eyebrow but listens. If Hank has a way for him to stop feeling like his heart's getting run through a shredder every day, he's all ears.

"You should talk to him about this. Spell it out for him. You might have to be a little bit brave, but it'll be worth it."

"That's your brilliant advice? Talk to him?"

Hank's apparently not offended at Ryan's incredulous tone. "You might be surprised what happens. That boy may be dumb, but he's not stupid. Who wouldn't jump at a chance to be with you, Ryan?"

Hank's gaze slides away from Ryan and his mouth goes lopsided and Ryan feels like a jerk all over again. He sidesteps one trap and falls into another.

"I know Jesse cares about me. But he doesn't—he'll never feel the way about me that I feel about him. You don't know what he's been like lately, always trying to set me up with other guys. Why would he do that if he had any feelings for me other than that ridiculous sense of responsibility he took on when he saved my life? I'm just an obligation to him. Someone he stands by because he's the most loyal guy on the planet." He knows he sounds bitter, and he knows Hank doesn't deserve to be mixed up in this one-sided drama. He sighs. "You're being way too nice to me, Hank. If I were you, I'd wish we'd never come to Pine Tree Lodge."

The doctor reaches out, puts a hand on Ryan's shoulder. "I'll never be sorry you two walked through my door."

Ryan's eyes inexplicably fill with tears. He leans into Hank's touch, wishing for the hundredth time that he could just switch his feelings for Jesse to someone like Hank with the snap of his fingers.

"I'm sorry I'm such a mess," he whispers.

"Hey, it's going to be all right. Think about what I said about talking to him? Please?" Hank squeezes Ryan's shoulder then lets go. "I've got to go to the clinic, but you have my number. Use it if you need to." He smiles a little. "Or even if you just want to. Okay?"

Ryan blinks away the moisture in his eyes before a single humiliating tear is able to fall. "Okay."

Hank nods and stands. "Now, eat your breakfast. Those biscuits are better warm."

Ryan watches Hank go out the back way by the kitchen, his mind swirling with doubt. Talk to Jesse?

There are so many things that could go wrong. He's about to dig into the Lodge Special which has surely gone cold by now but stops with his fork halfway to his mouth. Jesse's standing in the entrance to the great room, his gaze fixed on the exit Hank just used, and he's scowling.

EIGHT

JESSE MAKES his way to Ryan's table—the same one Jesse chose yesterday, randomly—and sits down in the seat Hank just vacated.

"What's wrong?" Ryan asks, his eyebrows drawn together. "Are you okay?"

"Am I—Ryan, are you okay? Did Hank do something? Have you—have you been *crying*?" Ryan's eyes are rimmed with red and ringed with shadows. He'd arrived at the lodge in time to see Hank put his hand on Ryan's shoulder and then book it, while Ryan sat looking like someone had delivered bad news. Jesse's initial worry at waking to find Ryan gone from the cabin had morphed into concern that Hank had done something villainous. And it would all be Jesse's fault.

Ryan blinks rapidly and clears his throat. "No, I'm fine. And Hank didn't do anything."

"Are you sure? I'm pretty sure I could take him," Jesse says, not convinced that Ryan isn't lying, and not sure why this has him so off-kilter. He ignores the small yet persistent voice in the back of his head that tells him he *does* know.

Ryan smiles at Jesse's bravado. "That won't be necessary. Hank is—" He looks in the direction where Hank had disappeared, and his smile softens. Jesse shivers as if someone's touched the back of his neck with an ice cube. "Hank is a good man," Ryan finishes quietly.

"Oh." Jesse doesn't know what to say. Of course Hank is a good man. Jesse worked with him for two years. Not always that closely, but he had a great reputation, and he's been nothing but good to them since they arrived in Columbia. He's a damn saint, really, taking on the medical care of everyone in this remote part of Vermont.

Ryan deserves someone like that in his life. Jesse feels small and petty. "Sorry. I guess I was worried when I woke up and you weren't there."

"I am over eighteen the last time I checked my driver's license," Ryan says dryly. "Pretty sure I can manage to feed myself breakfast. Was going to bring you back some, too."

"Right. Of course. Thanks," Jesse says. He seems to always be on the wrong foot lately. Being tired and hungry doesn't help. He didn't have the best night of sleep in the world, taking ages to fall asleep, and then once he did, he had anxiety dreams about getting up on stage to perform and not remembering any of the lyrics to the songs he'd written himself, while Ryan watched from the wings, shaking his head in disappointment.

He can fix his exhaustion with coffee. Now, how to address the hunger?

Right on cue, Joy stops by their table with a Lodge Special. "Saw you come in and figured you'd want this," she says, delivering it with a smile. "And extra marmalade."

"Joy, you are a beacon of light in a dark world," Jesse says.

"I know. Back in a second with coffee."

Jesse takes an enormous bite of flakey, buttery biscuit, and groans. His day is looking up. It takes him a second to register that Ryan's not eating, hasn't touched his breakfast, by the looks of it. He's just watching Jesse with an unreadable expression. "What?" he says with his mouth full.

Ryan opens his mouth, closes it, opens it again. "Have you ever—" He snaps his mouth shut again.

Jesse swallows. "What?" he says again, more clearly this time.

But Ryan just shakes his head. "Eat your breakfast. We need our strength if we're going to start working on the album today." He picks up his fork and begins to eat quickly, as if he's only just remembered he's ravenous.

Jesse follows his lead, but he wonders what Ryan was going to say.

"WE'VE GOT to stop missing lunch," Jesse moans. It's four o'clock in the afternoon and his stomach is empty. After breakfast, they'd started talking about a list of songs to cover and that discussion had taken them back to the cabin, where they'd gotten out their guitars and jammed for a while, all the weirdness of the last forty-eight hours fading away as he and Ryan do what they do best—make music.

They argued over a few songs and agreed on a few more. Turns out Ryan has surprisingly passionate opinions about "The Christmas Song" while Jesse went to bat for "Rockin' Around the Christmas Tree." They both agreed that "O Holy Night" is kind of a no-brainer, especially if they go with the spare, acoustic arrangement that Jesse has in mind. Ryan sang it slow and sweet and the goosebumps that rose on Jesse's arm at Ryan's almost holy voice haven't yet fully gone away.

"Early dinner?" he asks as they stand and stretch, then put away their guitars.

Ryan checks his phone. He gets a little smile on his face and taps out a short text before looking up. Who is he texting? Hank?

"Yeah. Should we go see what Columbia, Vermont, has to offer?"

"Sounds good. I'll get my jacket."

He goes to his room, looks at himself in the mirror. He wonders if he should change out of the sweatshirt and jeans he's wearing. But that would be ridiculous. He doubts there's a dress code, and Ryan's wearing something similar. He runs a hand through his hair, realizes he hasn't shaved today. What's the big deal? Ryan knows what he looks like. It's not like Ryan's suddenly going to look at him and think—

Jesse has to grab the edge of the dresser for support when the realization hits him. Ryan isn't going to just look at him one day and see someone he'd *want*. He's got a touch of vertigo at his own stupidity. It's not like he wants Ryan to want him. Does he?

He lets go of the dresser slowly, forces himself to turn away from the mirror and grab his warm jacket. There must be something in this Vermont air that's messing with his mind. He and Ryan are friends. Best friends. And despite both being technically the right gender for a possible physical relationship, that's never been on the table. At first, it was because Jesse wasn't about to screw up his opportunity to advance his music career, and then later, it was about them becoming true friends. Plus, they were always seeing other people, and it never came up.

But what if it had? Would Jesse have been interested?

The way he's been acting, or reacting, the last couple of days, makes him think that not only would he have been interested, but he *is* interested. In Ryan. Which is just weird. Not to mention pathetic.

Ryan's the most beautiful person Jesse's ever known. He's got a voice like a fallen angel, a face like a naughty one. He's hard to get to know but once you're in, he's loyal and kind to his core. Ryan is so far out of Jesse's league, he still wakes up and can't believe that Ryan talks to him, let alone cares about him, wants to work with him. He lucked into this and on some level, he keeps expecting his luck to run out.

When he meets Ryan at the door to the cabin, and Ryan smiles at him. Jesse's heart flip flops in his chest; he's pretty sure the sand is running out of the top of the hourglass. Everything's about to get turned upside down.

And unless he stops this nonsense he's going to get banged up in the process.

"You want me to look for a spot or just drive and see what we find?" Ryan asks as they walk to their rental SUV. "Hank mentioned an Asian fusion place. He said to stay away from the Italian place by the train tracks. Apparently, it's bad."

"Uh, yeah, let's just go," Jesse says. He nearly forgot about Hank in his mini-freakout. It doesn't matter how he feels, it only matters how Ryan feels. And it seems like Ryan has feelings for Hank. Which is just dandy.

"Is everything okay?" Ryan asks, side eyeing him.

"Uh, yeah. I'm just hungry."

"Okay. Want me to drive?"

"Nah," Jesse says, trying for his usual nonchalance. "I got it."

It's only a five-minute drive from the lodge to what passes for downtown Columbia. There's a single main street with a few cross streets, a couple of stop lights, and then civilization tapers off into rural roads.

"There's Hank's clinic." Ryan points out a squat gray building next to a dentist's office and across the street from a pharmacy. There's a tiny used bookshop and a coffee shop and a smattering of clothing stores on the next block.

By the time they get to the end of the main drag, they realize their choices are Mexican, Asian, and a diner. After a short debate, they decide on the diner since it's the one most likely to be open at this time of day.

"What sounds good to you?" Jesse asks once they settle into a booth by the window. He's almost too hungry to decide, and he's basically going to ask the server to choose something for him, when he realizes Ryan's not even looking at the menu, but at his phone again.

"Something urgent?" Jesse asks.

"Huh?" Ryan looks up, distracted. "No, it's Hank. He says the chicken fried steak is good here."

"Well, if Hank said it, then obviously that's what we should order." Jesse winces as he hears the sarcasm in his voice.

"Seriously, what is up with you? Hank has been nothing but nice to us since we got here," Ryan says sharply.

"Nothing," Jesse mutters. How can he tell Ryan the only reason he's pissy about Hank is because Ryan seems to like him so much? Not only does that make him the biggest hypocrite on the planet, after spending the last six months trying to set Ryan up, but it would only lead to questions he's not prepared to answer. "Chicken fried steak. Great."

"You love chicken fried steak," Ryan says, still puzzled.

"I know. So I'm ordering it. Let's just drop it." Jesse immediately feels bad when Ryan's expression shutters. God, he's such an asshole. Jesse's inconvenient feelings aren't Ryan's problem. Ryan fiddles with his napkin and he wants to touch his hand, to reassure him that just because Jesse's having some weird "Ryan is hot" phase, it doesn't change anything. But he keeps his hands to himself, orders the chicken fried steak as graciously as possible. Ryan orders a chicken Caesar salad, and they both order coffee.

"You wanna hear a song I've been working on when we get back to the lodge?" Jesse asks, both to change the subject and get his mind on something that makes sense—work.

"Sure, Jess." Ryan's still fiddling with his napkin and Jesse wonders what Hank texted to him. More than just a dinner recommendation, he'd wager.

"So, uh, you know how Hank was at breakfast this morning?"

"Yeah."

"He was asking me about, that is, he brought up something that—" Ryan sighs. "He was giving me some advice and I've been thinking about it all day."

"Advice about what?" Jesse tries not to feel stung that Ryan's been able to talk with Hank about something he isn't able to talk with Jesse about.

"Well, about something that's been on my mind a lot lately. For a long time now. It's gotten to be distracting so he thinks I need to get it off my chest. Only it's not that simple. I don't think so, anyway." Ryan doesn't look at Jesse while he compulsively straightens his silverware.

"Okay. Well, he's probably right. Just letting stuff fester isn't healthy." Jesse wants to bang his head on the table. If this new awareness of Ryan doesn't go away, he's going to be the one with the festering secret. He reminds himself this conversation is about Ryan, not him, and refocuses on his friend. "So what's on your mind?"

Ryan takes a deep breath. His cheeks go a little pink.

The word adorable flits across Jesse's mind. No, not adorable. Just Ryan being Ryan. Argh.

"I don't know if I can—I don't really have the right words," he says haltingly.

"Maybe you should write it down," Jesse says.

"Huh?"

"You're an amazing writer, Ryan. Maybe you need to write it, not say it."

Ryan frowns. "I sort of have," he mutters, but then he looks up and meets Jesse's gaze for the first time since they sat down at the table. His blue eyes shine. "Actually, I haven't written a—" He stops, touches his fork, takes another breath. "Yeah, that's a good idea. Thanks, Jess."

Ryan's smile is warm and melts Jesse from the inside out. He has no idea what Ryan's talking about, only that he said something right. He'll take it, and he'll try to shove these inappropriate feelings back where they came from. Only trouble is, he's never been that great at hiding what he feels, especially not from Ryan.

THE NEXT DAY they wake up around the same time and head to the main building for breakfast together. Ryan can feel his arteries protesting all the butter he's been consuming, so he gets oatmeal and an egg white omelet, while Jesse stuffs his face with the Lodge Special for the third day in a row.

Ryan's feeling pretty good, all things considered. Some of the exhaustion from the tour is finally lifting after sleeping soundly the night before. He's cleared the air with Hank, who's texted him a few friendly messages since yesterday's breakfast. It's nice to feel like he has a friend he can talk about Jesse with if he needs to. And he's definitely been thinking about what Hank said about talking to Jesse himself.

He's considering it, but he's worried the words will get stuck in his throat and he'll chicken out. Instead, he thinks maybe the solution lies in writing a song. He's written a half dozen down-beat ballads in recent months, but he's hasn't written an honest-to-god love song, where he puts his heart on the line and asks someone to be his. That's what keeps kicking around in his head. Maybe he doesn't have to talk to Jesse. Maybe he can just sing to him.

Either way, today he doesn't need anything besides being in this beautiful place with his best friend, noodling around on their guitars.

The more relaxed Ryan is, the jumpier Jesse seems to get, though. Despite claiming that everything is fine, Jesse seems distracted. He's rubbing the scar on his arm more than usual, and every time Ryan claps him on the shoulder he jumps like a skittish cat.

They get delivery of pad Thai and fried rice for lunch, and it's not until they're cleaning up that Ryan realizes something else is off about Jesse. He hasn't touched him all day. Usually Ryan can't keep Jesse off him, he's always tapping his arm or nudging him with his foot when he wants to show him something. But Jesse's kept distance between them all day. It's weird.

Ryan muses on it all afternoon as they tweak one of Jesse's contributions to the Christmas album, a goofy novelty tune about Tennessee Santa delivering all the presents in a pickup truck. Why would Jesse keep himself to his side of the living room, with a large coffee table between them?

A dark thought enters his head, ruining his good mood. Does Jesse know? Is that why he's been keeping to himself? Ryan could see Jesse doing something like that to avoid giving Ryan false hope. Which is utterly depressing. But how would Jesse find out? It's not like Ryan has a diary with Mr. Ryan Arlyn written out in cursive letters that Jesse could accidentally find or anything like that. The only human being who knows about Ryan's feelings is Hank Moore, and as far as Ryan knows, Jesse doesn't even have Hank's number.

He's being paranoid. Chalk this up as another reason Hank's advice isn't terrible. If he tells Jesse, then Jesse will know, which could be bad, but at least it's out there. Ryan wouldn't have to keep living with the fear that Jesse will find out. And he supposes there's some sliver of a chance that if he does tell him, Jesse's reaction won't be a kindly let down or a horrified no. He honestly doesn't let himself think about the idea of Jesse feeling the same way, or even being open to exploring a relationship with him, because it hurts too much to think about how good it could be.

And it could be so freaking amazing. He and Jesse already spend so much time together, he already knows the highs and lows of living with the guy, they know each other's families, they work better together musically than apart. But thinking about sleeping in the same bed as Jesse, about rolling over and seeing his face first thing in the morning, kissing him awake. Telling him how much he means to him and not having to couch it in words of friendship or creative partnership. That would be incredible. Not that Jesse's friendship isn't worth its weight in gold all on its own. Ryan will take the friendship any day of the week. Which circles him right back to the beginning—if friends is enough for Jesse, and Ryan would rather be friends than nothing at all, why rock the boat by bringing up his feelings?

Ryan sighs, and realizes he's completely tuned out of

what they're working on. Funny thing is, Jesse's not paying attention, either. He's staring out the window of the cabin at the view of the forest behind them, rubbing his arm again in the spot where he wears the scar from the explosion.

"Your arm bothering you?" Ryan asks.

Jesse jumps a few inches off the couch at the sound of Ryan's voice and fumbles his guitar so it almost slides off his lap and onto the ground. "Huh?"

"Your arm." Ryan nods at the arm in question, covered now by a blue and white checked shirt. "Does it hurt?"

"No, it doesn't hurt," Jesse says distantly, as if in his thoughts he'd been far away. He touches his left hand to the back of his right arm and then drops it when he realizes what he's doing. "Habit, I guess."

"Because if your arm hurts, we could get Hank to look at it."

Jesse stands up quickly, setting his guitar aside. "I told you it's fine," he says sharply, before walking toward the kitchenette and opening the fridge, then slamming it noisily.

"I'm going into town for a bit. You want anything?"

Ryan frowns. It's not like Jesse to be moody. That's his wheelhouse. He stands up and put his own instrument to the side.

"Got something on your mind, Jess?"

Jesse gives him a weak smile. "No—yeah—no."

"Well that clears it up." Ryan's trying to keep things light, but he wants to fold Jesse in his arms and try to help him through whatever's got him down.

"It's nothing. Well, not nothing, but. I think maybe I just need to be alone for a little while."

"Sure, okay." Ryan tries not to take that personally. "You wanna go grab us some dinner? I'll keep working on this melody."

Jesse nods. "Yeah. Sounds good. Any requests?"

Ryan thinks about their options. "Think Vermont tacos are any good?"

"Only one way to find out," Jesse says.

"And get some beer. That way if the tacos suck, we can wash them down with something better."

"You got it."

Jesse smiles enough to show one of his dimples before grabbing the car keys and his jacket.

Ryan stops himself from telling Jesse to drive safe. He's not the guy's mom. Or his boyfriend. After Jesse's gone, he pulls out his phone and looks at the last text from Hank from before lunch that Ryan hadn't had a chance to answer.

HANK

How's it going? Any progress?

Ryan thinks about how to respond before typing.

It's going okay. I'm thinking of writing him a song. Is that cheesy?

Only a couple of minutes pass before his phone dings.

I'm pretty sure a song would be speaking his language. But how long does it take to write a song? I'm thinking you need to get this off your chest sooner rather than later.

I have a tune that didn't work for another song that I think might be perfect. Now I just need the lyrics.

Awesome. Can I hear it? I work the second shift tomorrow. Want to meet up for brunch?

Where?

You're welcome to come over.

Sounds good.

Jesse went out to pick up dinner. Do you want to come over and eat with us tonight?

Thanks, but I can't. I'm on a break but I'll be at the clinic until 9.

OK. See you tomorrow.

See you tomorrow, Ryan. ;-)

Ryan smiles and sets aside his phone. If he's going to run his song by Hank tomorrow, he ought to work on it while he has the cabin to himself. He starts strumming the tune, humming along. Usually he writes the melody to a song first before finding words to fit. He thinks about Jesse, about what he means to him. He thinks about how to tell his best friend that he loves him. But not just as a friend. As more than a friend.

"I wanna be more than friends," he sings softly. "My heart's on the line. I could be yours, and you could be mine."

They're not the most original words in the world, but he scribbles them down anyway, in the notebook where he keeps his song ideas and music notations before they get transferred into the computer app he uses to polish songs. He keeps working, lost in the verses and his feelings when the door to the cabin opens and Jesse walks in with a paper bag under each arm.

Ryan snaps the notebook shut and hurries to set down his guitar. "Back so soon?"

"I've been gone for two hours," Jesse says with a quizzical look on his face.

"Really?" Ryan can see that it's full on dark outside now. He stands up; his legs and back feel stiff. "Guess I lost track of time."

"Working hard? Can I hear it?" Jesse asks as he walks to the kitchenette.

Ryan can smell spices and suddenly realizes he's ravenous. "Uh. Hear what?"

"Whatever you were working on when I came in," Jesse says.

"Not yet."

Jesse doesn't seem bothered by Ryan's answer. He unloads the first bag. "I got tacos. Lots of tacos. Plus chips and salsa and beans and rice and gauc. I know we were skeptical, but this place seems legit."

"Smells amazing."

"And," Jesse pulls two six packs out of the other bag with a flourish, "there's more where this came from, too. I have to get the other bag out of the car."

"Sweet," Ryan says. "But I'm probably only good for one or two."

"What?" Jesse pouts, apparently out of whatever funk he'd been in before. "I thought we could put a movie on one of laptops and turn our brains off for a while."

"I'm in, I just don't want to overdo it. I'm going to meet up with Hank for brunch tomorrow and I don't want to be hungover."

Jesse turns around abruptly and puts the beer in the fridge. "Brunch? Like, a date?"

"No," Ryan says quickly. "Just a friends thing. I mean, you could come, too, probably."

Jesse stands up, throws Ryan an inscrutable look. "Nah. That sounds fun for you two. Maybe I'll go for a hike or something."

"Okay. But the movie's a good idea. I'll set that up if you want to do the food?"

"Deal."

Twenty minutes later they're settled on the couch, Ryan's laptop playing *The Hangover* and diving into the above-average Mexican food. Ryan's nursing a beer but Jesse cracks open his second before the guys in the movie even make it to Las Vegas. By the time the credits roll, Jesse's made his way through a six-pack all by himself and he's laughing so hard at the photo montage at the end that he's doubled over, his long body literally folded in half. Ryan's heart is light seeing Jesse cracking up at a movie they've both seen at least a dozen times.

When Jesse comes up for air, he's got tears in the corners of his eyes.

"You all right there, Jess?" Ryan asks, patting his shoulder.

"Shit, I love this movie."

"I know you do, buddy." Ryan closes the laptop and is about to ask Jesse if he wants some water, when suddenly Jesse's right there, in his space. Closer than they've been all day.

"Ryan."

Ryan waits, but Jesse doesn't say anything except his name. This close, he can see Jesse's irises turn from slate gray to almost silver. "Yeah?" His voice sounds low to him, but Jesse doesn't flinch.

"Ryan. Can I—I just need to know if—"

And then before Ryan can say anything or do anything or even lick his lips or take an extra breath, Jesse kisses him.

It's closed mouthed and little off center, but it still sends chills down Ryan's spine. Jesse is kissing him. They're mouth to mouth, and this isn't anything they've ever done before. Not together.

He's got about a million thoughts all battling for first place in his mind but before he can choose between pushing Jesse away and asking what the fuck is going on or deepening the kiss and finding out what Jesse actually tastes like under the flavor of beer, he's gone.

Jesse yanks himself back and stands up, leaving Ryan swaying alone on the couch.

"Okay, yeah. Sorry. Um. I'm going to go to bed," Jesse babbles.

Wait, Ryan wants to say, but Jesse practically sprints to his room and shuts the door with a loud bang.

So much for his first kiss with the man he loves.

TEN

JESSE THROWS himself face up on the bed, sticks a hand down his pants and closes it around his hard cock. Even drunk, just the merest taste of Ryan has gotten him all the way there in about five seconds. He strokes himself roughly, getting frustrated after a minute. This would feel so much better if it was Ryan's hand. Or Ryan's mouth. Or even if Ryan just let Jesse rut against him, his warm, soft body smelling of clean laundry and his favorite body wash. Yeah, maybe Ryan would have let Jesse kiss him and rub off on him and—Jesse comes to that, spilling into his hand, his head swimming, heart hammering in his chest.

He is such an idiot. Not only does he want Ryan, physically, but he'd actually kissed him. He'd kissed his best friend. And it was a *bad* kiss.

Jesse's an amazing kisser, in his humble opinion. And now Ryan probably thinks he's dismally below average. Fuck.

Jesse has no one to blame but himself for this tragic

turn of events. He's the one who thought alcohol would make the rabbity feeling in his chest go away after spending the entire day trying not stare at Ryan's nimble fingers on the frets of his guitar, trying not to grin at him like a lovesick fool at all of his suggestions about the album.

The thing is, Jesse has never been attracted to someone he cares about as much as he cares about Ryan. Of course he's had warm feelings for his girlfriends and boyfriends in the past. He always *likes* the people he hooks up with. But he's never had a physical relationship with someone he knows as well as Ryan. The combination of how much he already cares about his friend with this newfound awareness of him as a potential hook-up is uncharted territory and it's fucking with Jesse's head.

Three hours earlier, the answer had presented itself to him with such perfect clarity—alcohol. He'd realized that the root of all his problems was that he didn't know if he actually wanted to kiss Ryan or if he only *thought* he wanted to kiss him. Maybe kissing Ryan would be like kissing a sibling. Maybe it would be so prosaic and underwhelming that Jesse could chalk up his recent feelings to tour-induced exhaustion and he could move on with his life with Ryan as his best friend who was objectively attractive but he didn't want to have anything to do with sexually, thank you very much.

His plan had made so much sense when he and Ryan were sprawled on the coach, full of tacos and beer and watching one of their favorite movies. He'd simply kiss Ryan to find out if what he thought he felt for him was real or not. Simple.

Jesse is such a dumbass.

His mistake was to forget about Ryan's mouth. His lips, specifically. They're kind of made for kissing, so he's not sure why he thought that actually kissing them would be a turnoff. He'd screwed up his courage to try to find out one way or the other if this was all in his head, had touched his lips to Ryan's perfect ones, and had suffered the instantaneous head rush of having all his blood flee for parts south. The shock of how good a simple, chaste, off-center kiss felt understandably freaked him out.

Which is how he ended up in his bed, alone, frantically jerking off and consumed with regret the second his orgasm receded.

Great job, Arlyn, he chides himself. Way to make the situation fifty times worse.

Now he knows two things without a doubt. The first is that he definitely has sexual feelings for Ryan. But that's moot, because after that shocking display in there, the second thing he is 100 percent sure of is that Ryan is never going to want to let his mouth anywhere near him again.

Jesse groans, kicks off his pants and sticky boxers and throws his comforter over his head. He hopes his future self will be able to handle the aftermath of his past self's fuckup, because all his present self wants to do is sleep.

THAT NIGHT, he dreams about the land mine explosion.

It filters into his subconscious occasionally, but it's

probably been six months since the last time he can remember dreaming about it.

It's usually a variation on a theme. He's in the SUV. He's watching as the vehicle in front of them suddenly leaps into the air, becoming engulfed in flames. Sometimes he's stuck in his seat, unable to get out, unable to help the people in the flaming wreck. Sometimes the vehicle explodes before he can get to it.

Tonight is one of the worst versions of the dream. He's able to get to the other SUV, can see Ryan beyond the glass, unmoving, bleeding from his head wound. Jesse yells and screams and tries to get the door open and he can't. He tries everything to get to Ryan and he's powerless. He knows time is running out, that if he can't open the door, Ryan's going to die. That he'll lose him forever. He yanks at the door handle with all his might, and then Ryan's eyes fly open, his blue irises boring into him for one second before the second explosion happens.

Jesse jerks awake, the sensations of the dream so real he pats at his arms, until he realizes he's not on fire.

But he is alone. He squints at the clock. It's late morning. As the nightmare recedes, the memory of last night's pathetic display filters back in. He flops back on the bed, rubbing his eyes. He still can't believe he was so stupid as to kiss Ryan. No preamble. No dialogue. No, "Hey Ryan, so I've been thinking, and I'd like to kiss you. Would you be up for it? No? That's cool."

More than kissing him badly, he'd kissed Ryan without asking, a detail he'd conveniently avoided thinking about last night.

He owes his friend about six different apologies

before he can even start to think about telling Ryan about this newfound attraction he's feeling.

That is, if Jesse should even say anything at all. It's not Ryan's fault Jesse's suddenly lost his grip. It's Jesse's problem. He can deal with it on his own.

He's uneasy, though. Maybe it's the aftereffects of the bad dream, but he's anxious as he takes a quick, scalding hot shower and dresses for the day in jeans and a warm flannel. Whatever he's feeling, his number one priority is always making sure Ryan's okay. And he only has himself to blame if Ryan's spiraling.

He peeks his head out of his room cautiously. Ryan's door is closed. Maybe he's still asleep. He creeps into the living room. The coffee table where they ate dinner and watched the movie last night is clear. Not even an empty beer can betrays last night's activities. Their guitars are neatly stowed away. The kitchen is cleaned up, too. He opens the fridge to see a box of leftovers. He's strangely relieved to see them, otherwise he might start thinking he'd imaged the last twenty-four hours.

There's one more thing—a note written in Ryan's familiar blocky hand.

Having brunch with Hank. See you later. —R

Jesse's glad Ryan is communicating with him. But his relief at the apparent normalcy conflicts with a flare of jealousy. Ryan's seeing Hank—Jesse belatedly remembers he'd mentioned his plans last night. So it's not like

Jesse kissing Ryan drove him to see the doctor. And Ryan said it wasn't a date. But it's *something*. Jesse can feel it. And one bad, nonconsensual kiss doesn't change the fact that Ryan should be with someone as awesome as Hank.

Jesse stomach roils. He imagines going alone to the lodge for breakfast and the queasiness gets worse. He sets about making himself a cup of coffee in the kitchenette, mind racing as fast as his pulse. What on earth is he going do?

He sits down with his mug in the living room and stares out the cabin's big picture window onto the woods beyond. A hike sounds good. He needs to clear his head. And yet, the uneasy feeling about Ryan won't go away. He could text him, right? Just to make sure he's okay.

Or maybe he should give him some space. He's with Hank, who's basically the most competent person they know. The nightmare was only in Jesse's head. Ryan's fine. Jesse got to him in time six years ago. He'd escaped with nothing worse than a concussion.

Jesse remembers Ryan visiting him in the hospital when he was recovering from the surgery on his arm. He'd been so serious. So seriously beautiful, Jesse remembers, even through the haze of pain meds. Ryan had said if there was anything he could do for Jesse, Jesse only had to ask. Jesse had asked him for the thing he wanted most in the world. He had no idea then that the greatest thing Ryan was giving him wasn't an entryway into the music business.

He was giving Jesse his best friend.

So what if Jesse suddenly wants Ryan with a fierceness that shocks him? It doesn't matter. He won't hurt

Ryan ever again. He hopes Ryan can forgive him that one drunken kiss. He can't lose his best friend. He'll spend the rest of his life making it up to him if he has to. Their relationship doesn't have to change. He can live with keeping his feelings to himself. He'll have to.

ELEVEN

"MORE COFFEE?"

Ryan considers Hank's offer, then decides he's had enough coffee to keep him awake until Christmas. "No, thanks."

Hank nods and puts the pot down. They're sitting in Hank's kitchen, having put away half of the spinach mushroom quiche Hank liberated from the lodge's kitchen and a couple of blueberry muffins apiece. Hank's been telling him about work at the clinic and about some plans he and Emma have for the lodge, while Ryan does his best to pay attention and not think about the thing he's been thinking about for the past twelve hours straight.

"So are you going to tell me what happened or are you going for the championship in repressing your feelings?" Hank asks dryly.

Ryan twists his mouth into a rueful smile. "Sorry. I'm trying not to be bad company—"

"Ryan, you could never be bad company," Hank says lightly. "But I can tell there's something on your mind."

"Jesse kissed me last night." He blurts it out before he can reconsider.

Hank blinks. "Oh. Well—that's good, right?" He sounds slightly puzzled, but not hurt.

Ryan realizes he's been holding back from talking to Hank about this even though Hank's been nothing but supportive because he doesn't want to hurt the guy. He still feels bad about kissing him for the wrong reasons the other night, though Hank truly doesn't seem to be holding it against him.

"It was—weird," Ryan answers. He's not sure he didn't half dream it. "We were working on the album, and then Jesse went out and came back with takeout and beer. I was working on the song, the one, well, for him." His cheeks warm.

Hank smiles. "You're writing him a song. That's great. How's it coming?"

Ryan considers. He usually plays the early versions of his songs for Jesse, who gives him notes. It might not be a bad idea to run the song by another pair of ears. He certainly doesn't want to serenade Jesse with something half-baked, not if he's going to tell Jesse how he feels. "It's going all right, but it needs a polish. Would you be up for listening to it and telling me what you think?"

Hank chuckles. "I can't pretend I have any talent for anything musical."

"But you're an amazing listener," Ryan says honestly. "I'd love your opinion."

"Then I'd love to hear the song." Hank's so easy and

so kind and Ryan wishes again that he wasn't in love with someone else.

"So how did the kiss happen?" Hank asks. "I guess it didn't lead to talking, or anything else for that matter, or you probably wouldn't be so distracted."

"Uh, well, we watched a movie and Jesse got kind of sloppy on the beer, and we were on the couch, and he just said, well, he didn't say much. And then he kissed me. Then he ran to his room and slammed the door. I haven't seen him since." Ryan's heart is beating fast from reliving the brief encounter.

"Holy hell you two are hopeless," Hank grumbles. "You need to talk to each other. Why didn't you go after him?"

"I don't know." Ryan's been asking himself the same thing. "I don't know why he kissed me, but what if he did it as an experiment and never wants to do it again?"

Hank levels him with a look. "And you? Now that you've kissed him, do you want to do it again?"

"It was over so fast; I didn't really have time to react. It wasn't a real kiss," Ryan says, his voice rising. "He can't decide it's not going to be good between us based on one mediocre kiss. I didn't have time to prepare."

Hank looks like he's trying very hard not to laugh. Ryan would protest but the man's got a right.

"I'm just confused. Until last night, I thought my feelings were totally one-sided." Ryan swallows, almost afraid to say the next bit. Hank patiently waits for him to finish, no judgement in his eyes. "But maybe—maybe Jesse has feelings for me, too?"

Hank doesn't say anything and Ryan about jumps out of his skin waiting for the verdict.

"Well? Am I just seeing what I want to see?" he asks a bit desperately.

"I think if Jesse only saw you as a friend he wouldn't have kissed you." Hank shakes his head. "What you two need is to be locked in a room together until you work this out."

"We only have a few days left before we're supposed to fly home for Christmas." Ryan stands up and starts pacing. "We have more work to do on the album, and I'm writing this song, but I have no idea how to tell him—I mean, it was one thing when I was just stupidly pining for my best friend, but what if he—what if he—" He rubs his chest, anxiety forming a tight ball under his sternum.

"What if he feels the same way?" Hank finishes for him, voice devastatingly gentle. He smiles, crow's feet creasing the corners of his eyes. "Well, then, you'll be one of those lucky people who fall in love with someone who loves them back."

"Why is the idea of that so scary?" Ryan whispers.

"Why did you join the Peace Corps, Ryan?"

The change in subject stops Ryan's agitation. "I—I wanted to give something back." He's answered this question five dozen times in interviews over the years. "My debut album did unexpectedly well, and I felt like I needed to contribute something to the world besides a few radio hits."

"But why did you really join?" Hank asks, still smiling, but there's a harder edge to his question now.

Ryan sighs. Damn the man for being so perceptive.

"I wanted to get away. From myself. From the fame, the money, the stress of interacting with fans. I was an out, gay country star with a gold album. There was so much attention on me, and it had nothing to do with playing music. All I ever wanted to do was write songs. Sing 'em. Maybe get paid to do it. I wasn't running away from the music. I was running from everything else. Maybe from myself, too."

Hank nods. He's probably heard a variation on this story more than once, with all his years in the Corps. Ryan's not unique. And running away hadn't helped him make peace with the industry he'd found himself in. Only working with Jesse did that. Jesse, who made him rediscover his love for performing, who runs interference with the press, with the fans, with the record company. Jesse, who's good at handling fame, and who still wants to make music with Ryan, even after finding out what a ball of neuroses he really is.

Jesse, who might want to be more than friends.

"I was trying to get away from something, and I ended up finding Jesse. And then together we faced a new adventure. I couldn't have made it through the past six years without him."

"Well, then, it makes sense you don't want to risk your relationship," Hank says reasonably. "Though I still think what the two of you have is strong enough to figure this out. Don't be afraid to lose him. And don't be afraid to win him, either. You deserve all the happiness in the world."

Ryan's eyes suddenly feel hot, and he swipes his

thumb over them hastily. "You a part time therapist, too, Hank?"

The doctor shrugs. "I like to help my friends."

"We're practically strangers," Ryan protests.

"No, you're not." Hank stands up, checks his watch. "I need to run some errands in town. I'd ask if you want to join me, but I don't want you using me as an excuse to avoid Jesse."

Ryan scrunches up his face. "I'm not making excuses—okay, well maybe a little. Do you have time to listen to the song before you go? I could run and grab my guitar."

"Sure. Why don't I drive you to your cabin—unless you want to find Jesse and clear the air."

"It'll keep a little longer." Call him a coward, but he's not in a rush to explode his life.

They clear up their brunch dishes, and Hank leads him out a back door to a little carport on the far end of the lodge building. Ryan climbs into Hank's truck, a sturdy four-by-four with a covered bed.

In a minute, they've circled the lodge. Hank parks in front of cabin 14. Ryan opens up, half excited to see Jesse, half trepidatious. But the interior of the cabin is quiet and still.

"He's not here, I guess," Ryan says, partly relieved, partly disappointed.

"Come on, play for me," Hank says, perching on the arm of the couch. "I want to hear a real old-fashioned love song."

"Hey, that's not a bad title." Ryan grins and picks up his guitar, strumming it a little to warm up his fingers. He grabs his notebook and opens it, scribbles down a couple of new lines. He sits across from Hank in the armchair, his back to the door. "Let me know what you think."

He starts to the play, the melody coming easily, like an old friend. The lyrics are stickier. He hums the first verse, still warming up, then launches in.

> *I wanna be more than friends.*
> *My heart's on the line.*
> *I could be yours, and you could be mine.*
>
> *My love's not a gift.*
> *Not a spell or a curse.*
> *It's just how I feel, for better or worse.*
>
> *You're everything to me.*
> *But that's all it has to be.*
> *Could I be everything to you?*
> *Could it be that you want me, too?*
>
> *I wanna be more than friends.*
> *My heart's waiting to hear back.*
> *Could I be in love with someone who*
> > *loves me back?*

Ryan stops and lets the last notes die away. Hank's been looking at him the whole time, quiet and watchful, his toe tapping along to the rhythm.

"That last couplet needs some work," Ryan says before Hank can say anything. "I need a stronger rhyming word. Using back twice is lazy."

"You'll figure that out. It's a beautiful song, Ryan."

"Yeah?" Ryan smiles. "It's shaping up pretty nicely. Let me try that last verse again."

"Go for it," Hank says, his gaze darting behind Ryan, then back again.

Ryan focuses, not wanting to let the words slip away. He starts with the last verse, letting his voice ring out strong and clear.

> *I wanna be more than friends*
> *My heart's beating despite its cracks.*
> *Am I in love with someone who loves me*
> > *back?*

Ryan stops singing, frowns down at his fingers. Is that the right lyric? He's about to jot the variation down just in case, when he notices Hank looking behind him again.

"Hey, Jesse," Hank says.

Ryan whirls around in the chair. Jesse is, indeed, standing there, looking like he's just come in from the cold with a beanie over his hair and a cherry red nose. His mouth is shaped into what's probably supposed to look like a smile.

"Hank," Jesse says unenthusiastically. "Hey. How was your brunch?"

"It was made better by the wonderful company," Hank says, shooting a smile Ryan's way before standing up. "Well, I'd be happy to listen to you all day, Ryan, but I have to go run those errands."

Ryan stands up, too, bringing the guitar with him.

He's an inch away from begging Hank not to leave, because then he'd be forced to follow through on that talking to Jesse thing. His stomach jumps—he's as nervy as if he's about to perform in front of thousands of people.

Hank must sense his panic, because he claps a strong, reassuring hand on his shoulder, squeezes, then pulls him in for a brief hug. Before he lets go, he whispers, "Talk to him. Trust me."

Ryan can't do anything but nod tightly. Then Hank's gone, and Jesse's standing there, his face tight and unreadable.

He knows he's supposed to do something. To say something. To play something? He's got his guitar in his hand. But the song's not quite right, not yet. But before he can do anything, Jesse's talking.

"You were playing for Hank?" It's not an accusation, but there's still a note of hurt in Jesse's voice.

"Uh. Yeah. Sort of."

"Didn't recognize the song."

"It's a new one," Ryan says, feeling strangely defensive. This isn't going the way it's supposed to. "Needed to get a second opinion."

"Oh." And now Jesse sounds...sad? "I—are you all right?"

"Huh? I'm fine. I'm glad you're here." There, that's a statement that resembles a conversation opener.

"You are?" Jesse says faintly. "I've been out walking around the woods."

"You want to come in, sit down for a minute?" Look at him, being a grown up.

Jesse peels the beanie off his head, leaving behind a bird's nest of dark hair. He runs a hand through it in a futile attempt to smooth it down, then comes all the way into the room. "Sure, of course. We need to talk."

"Yes!" Ryan's so relieved they seem to be on the same page, he can't help his smile. But as Jesse shrugs out of his jacket, Ryan suddenly realizes how thirsty he is. He sets down his guitar, retreats to the kitchenette and fills a glass with water from the tap.

"Want anything?" he calls.

"Nah," Jesse answers, sounding distracted.

He drinks down half the glass, vaguely wishing it wasn't the middle of the day so he could pour himself something stronger. Then again, even alcohol probably wouldn't give him the courage he needs to get through this conversation. When he turns back to the living room, his blood goes cold. Jesse's bent over the armchair, peering at Ryan's notebook, which he'd left open on the page with his lyrics for Jesse's song.

He crosses the room quickly, putting his hand over the pages and shutting the notebook. "That's—the song's not ready yet."

"Okay. Sorry for looking. You've never minded me— never mind." Jesse slumps down onto the couch, shoulders rounded in.

"It's okay." Ryan should probably use this as an opening. He could say *yeah, I'm working on a love song. For you. Because I'm in love with you. How do you feel about me?* That's probably the kind of mature, clear communication Hank had in mind.

Unfortunately, Ryan is still Ryan. "So, how was your

walk?" He cringes at the banal question, but Jesse doesn't seem to be paying attention anyway.

"Look, Ryan. I'm sorry for looking at your lyrics. And I'm sorry for last night. Really, truly, I can't believe I did that without asking you. I was drunk. And not thinking clearly. So I'm sorry. I really hope you can forgive me, and we can stay friends."

"Stay friends?" Jesus. Ryan's suddenly not sure he can do this. Jesse's worried about them staying friends over an impromptu kiss. What will he say if Ryan tells him he wants to do a lot more than that?

Jesse drops forward off the couch and onto his knees. He looks terrible, bloodshot eyes and hands clasped in front of him as if he's praying, or begging. Ryan sinks down in the armchair, so the height difference between them isn't so apparent. His heart is racing, his body not able to process the conflicting emotional inputs.

"I am so sorry," Jesse says again. "Your friendship is so important to me, Ryan. You have no idea how important. I wouldn't mess it up for anything, and reading those words, what you were singing to Hank—you have to know I wouldn't do anything to get in the way of you and Hank. Please tell me we're going to be okay."

Jesse looks so wretched; Ryan just wants to say whatever's going to take the look of anguish off his face. But one part doesn't make sense. "Get in the way of me and Hank?"

"Was it a love at first sight kind of thing? I get it—the beard's pretty sexy." Jesse's clearly trying for his usual insouciance but failing miserably.

Ryan's had about enough of this talking in circles.

Didn't Jesse just say their friendship was important to him? He had to believe it could survive Ryan's love confession. "I'm not in love with Hank," he says firmly. "And the song isn't for him. It's for—"

That's the moment a sharp rap comes on the cabin door. Jesse's gaze flies to the door, then back to Ryan, who shrugs. Housekeeping? He gets up to answer the door. But instead of a uniformed employee with a cart, he comes face to face with someone else.

"Cameron?"

TWELVE

JESSE SCRAMBLES TO HIS FEET. Did he hear
Ryan say *Cameron?*

Shit.

In all the unexpected drama of his new feelings for
Ryan and working on the album and renewing their
acquaintance with Hank, Jesse completely and utterly
forgot about Cameron Keane, Ryan's ex-boyfriend and
the reason he chose Pine Tree Lodge as their destination
in the first place.

He rushes to hover behind Ryan. Cameron, looking
tanned and healthy, his brown hair longer than Jesse's
own and tied back from his face, is smiling broadly, teeth
gleaming in the winter sun. He's a few years older than
Ryan, which puts him closer to Hank's age than Jesse's.

Jesse has always liked the guy. He's easy to get along
with, and he's the best keyboardist Jesse's ever met.
When he and Ryan were dating, he'd been happy that
the guy Ryan was spending so much time with was cool
and didn't seem to mind his and Ryan's friendship.

When Cameron left to go on an international tour, he and Ryan started hanging out at pre-Cameron levels, and Jesse had been selfishly glad, until Ryan started getting moody and writing sad, pining ballads all over the place. All signs pointed to Ryan missing Cameron. Jesse steels himself to go through with the original plan—if Ryan wants Cameron, well. Jesse wants Ryan to get what he wants. That hasn't changed, even if Jesse's feelings have.

"Ryan, aren't you a sight for sore eyes," Cameron says, sweeping Ryan into a back-slapping hug. "And Jesse, my man, good to see you."

Jesse finds himself on the receiving end of one of Cameron's hugs and he tries to smile back. "Hey, Cameron." He glances at Ryan, who looks surprised and something else. Jesse spends a second trying to figure out if Ryan is surprised-confused, or surprised-happy, or maybe even surprised-upset. He can't figure it out in the short window of time before someone has to stay something before the moment gets weird.

"What are you doing here?" Ryan asks, which is both logical and the last thing Jesse wants him to be asking.

Cameron rocks back on his heels. "I just got in after literally the flight—make that *flights*—from hell. I left Bangkok like four days ago, got stuck in Hong Kong, then there was a storm in Seattle. I was just about ready to rent a car and drive across the damn country, but I finally made it on a plane here."

"That sucks," Jesse says. He suddenly feels bad for forgetting that Cameron was supposed to be here days ago. He's always had tunnel vision when it comes to Ryan. Another clue that maybe he should have picked up on his feelings earlier. Well, he can't freak out now, even if his brain's still stuck on how Ryan was going to finish that sentence a few minutes earlier. Who did he write the song for, if not Hank? Is it Cameron? Is there someone *else* Ryan's been quietly seeing? Is the reason he's not interested in Hank or anyone else because he's already in a relationship?

Jesse shivers. He promised himself he'd be okay with Ryan never finding out how he feels, but it's not going to be easy to stand by and watch the best person Jesse knows bestow his love on someone else.

"Yeah, that sucks," Ryan agrees. "Uh. Well, it's nice to see you. You want to come in?"

"Sure," Cameron says. "I know I'm technically a Vermonter, but my blood's weak after all that time in the south." He walks into their cabin, and Ryan shuts the door.

"Right, you're from this area," Ryan says, as if dredging up the detail from the back of his mind. "What a coincidence."

Cameron gives him a funny look. "I'm from right here in Columbia. My parents live five minutes away. That's why I decided to stay at the lodge for the holidays. My folks just got a puppy and I need my beauty sleep. Plus, I always liked this big place. I worked here one summer in high school, even."

"You in a cabin?" Jesse asks, walking toward the kitchenette. "How was your tour? Are you hungry? Maybe we should order something." He's talking fast and rubbing his scar nervously.

Cameron turns his gaze on Jesse now, forehead

creased. "Am I interrupting something?" he asks. "I can come back later."

Yes. "No, this is great," Jesse says, cringing at the note of fake brightness in his voice. "We want to hear all about the tour."

Cameron doesn't seem convinced. Ryan folds his arms in front of him and looks at Jesse. His eyes are narrow, and Jesse suddenly feels like a kid being asked why there are a bunch of candy wrappers under his bed.

"How did you know we were here?" Ryan's asking Cameron, but his gaze hasn't left Jesse.

"When I told Jesse I was coming back to the States, that I'd be here over the holidays, Jesse said you two wanted to get away for a bit, said this place sounded perfect. We were supposed to meet here a few days ago, but, like I said, I got held up."

"That's why you chose Pine Tree Lodge, Jesse?" Ryan doesn't sound mad, but his hands are gripping his arms tightly.

"Yeah." He knows how it looks, how it sounds. Hell, maybe he deserves the look of ire Ryan's throwing his way.

"Didn't I tell you not to—you said there wouldn't be anybody—" Ryan literally throws up his hands. "You are unbelievable."

Jesse's seen Ryan mad before, but it's never been directed at him. Not like this. "I'm sorry," he says in a small voice. Meddling in Ryan's love life seemed a lot more harmless a few days ago. Now he wishes he'd never heard of Pine Tree Lodge.

"Um. Maybe I'll just see you guys later," Cameron says, edging toward the door.

"This entire trip was about Cameron? I can't believe I felt guilty for being suspicious. You must have been disappointed when he wasn't here, until, surprise, you could just throw me in the path of Hank. Great plan B." Ryan's well and truly angry now, his voice booming in the small cabin. "Please hear me when I tell you that just because you saved my life doesn't give you the right to run it."

Jesse wants to argue, to protest that he only had the best of intentions, but his intentions don't matter. "I know. I'm sorry." He looks at Cameron, who seems ready to bolt. "Jesus, I'm sorry, Cameron. I'm a complete idiot."

"Hey, no harm," Cameron says easily, "but maybe I'll leave you two to work this out."

What's to work out? Jesse messed up. He deserves Ryan's wrath.

"It's good to see you, Cameron," Ryan says, voice still sharp, making him sound very un-Ryan's like, "but yeah, I think Jesse and I need to talk."

Jesse's eyes widen. He wasn't expecting that. "You sure you don't—"

"You don't know what I want," Ryan says icily.

Right. He shoots Cameron a weak smile. "Sorry, man. Later?"

"Later," Cameron repeats. He looks between them for a beat. "For what it's worth, I hope you guys figure it out."

Jesse shivers, and not just from the cold air that comes inside as Cameron leaves the cabin.

With Cameron gone the cabin feels smaller than ever. Ryan's normally soft-as-your-favorite-blue-jeans eyes look hard as glass as he stares Jesse down.

Jesse doesn't know what to do. He's good at making Ryan feel better when it's an annoying record company employee or a tricky lyric giving him problems. He doesn't know how to solve the problem when the problem is *him*.

Ryan points at the couch. "Sit."

Jesse does as he's told, sinking onto the cushion where just last night he'd kissed Ryan. He closes his eyes. He couldn't have fucked this up any worse, could he?

"Now, listen to me," Ryan says. "That's all I ask. And then when I'm done, we might have to make some hard decisions. And I'll have to live with those consequences, but it'll be better than this, with me not in control of my own life. Okay?"

He doesn't know what Ryan means by decisions and consequences, but it doesn't sound good. On the other hand, what else can he do but agree? "Okay."

"I don't know where along the way things got so twisted that you thought you needed to be in charge of me, and I know it's mostly my fault. When I met you, I was looking for a way out, but you gave me a way back in, a way back to my life that made it...I don't know. Make sense. Making music made sense if you were making it with me. My life made sense with you there. And I guess it worked out okay for you, too—I mean, you got what you wanted. A music career. Fans. Money. Your songs on the radio. I had all those things, but they didn't mean anything until you joined the ride, Jesse."

Jesse's stunned. He knows he helped Ryan, but he hadn't realized Ryan felt this way.

"And all of that's great. It's more than great. I'm grateful for all of it. But somewhere I got it in my head, or you got it in your head, that I couldn't do it without you."

Ryan's been looming over him, but now he falls into the armchair heavily. "You've always been better than me at, well, everything, Jesse. I shouldn't have started relying on you so much. Maybe then you wouldn't feel like you literally have to get me a date. And maybe I've had some messed-up reasons for letting it get this far." He glances at his notebook, perched on the edge of the chair, then at Jesse. "But that stops now. I've been really scared, and confused, and it's all my damn fault. I've been avoiding this, but it's probably what needs to happen. We need to spend some time apart, Jesse."

"What? Why?" The panic crawls up Jesse's throat and he wants to jump in with a dozen reasons why not. But this is Ryan's show, and he forces himself to wait.

"Because that song I was writing? An old-fashioned love song," Ryan says scornfully, "it wasn't for Hank, or Cameron, or some guy I haven't met yet. It's for *you*, Jesse. I'm in love with you. I have been for a long time. And it's been really hard—" Ryan stops and takes a shallow breath and when he speaks again Jesse can hear the tears thickening his voice and it just about breaks his heart. "I don't think it's good for me to be around you right now. I'm sorry."

Jesse feels like he's trapped in one of those dreams where you're underwater and can't break the surface.

He's drowning in their Vermont cabin, unable to draw oxygen into his lungs. Dizzily, he lowers his head between his knees, vaguely registering Ryan's voice and then his presence, dropping onto the ground next to him, rubbing circles onto his back until he can finally take a full breath.

"It's okay, you're okay." Ryan murmurs nonsense and Jesse grabs onto his shirt, as if he can physically keep him from leaving. He tries to even out his breathing, and all he can smell is Ryan, and then his eyes burn because he's scared this is the last time Ryan will let him be this close.

"I'm—" Jesse tries and has to clear his throat and start over. "I'm so, so sorry that you've been hurting because of me." That's the most important thing, Jesse thinks. "When all you want is for someone to be happy and then you find out they're unhappy because of you, well, that's pretty rough. So I'm sorry."

"It's not your fault," Ryan says automatically. "You didn't know."

Jesse lifts his head. Ryan lets his hand that had been resting on Jesse's back fall away. They're as close as they were last night, and Jesse's hand is still clutched in Ryan's shirt. He doesn't want to let go. Not yet.

"I didn't know," he agrees, "but I shouldn't have done some of the things I did. I was an idiot. I want you to know that I never thought I knew better than you. I never wanted to control your life. I just—you're so amazing, and you're capable of amazing things, and I just thought that we were brought together for a reason and maybe that reason was so that I could help you, I don't know, be your amazing self? I guess that sounds self-aggrandizing in a way, but that's not how I thought about it."

"I know, Jesse. You've got a big heart and you included me in it, and it worked. It worked." Ryan's mouth twists. "But you forgot something. You're amazing, too. And I couldn't help falling for you. I wish I could have. I know my feelings are fucking everything up. Which is why it's better if I just—"

"Wait. I just have to ask you something," Jesse says, hoping he's not about to make a huge mistake. "After how I acted, with the set ups and coming here and trying to, well, I honestly was only trying to make you happy and I see now that I went about it completely the wrong way, but after all of that do you think you can forgive me?"

Ryan sighs. His eyes look soft again and Jesse thinks that's a good sign. "Of course, Jess. I forgive you."

Jesse's shoulders feel like two boulders have shifted off of them. "Thanks, Ryan." He lets himself think about the implications of the other things Ryan said. His feelings. Ryan said he's in love. With *him*.

Suddenly, Jesse registers exactly how close they are. He slowly lets go of Ryan's shirt, runs his hands over the wrinkled cloth, inadvertently, or perhaps not so inadvertently, running his hands over Ryan's chest. He pauses, letting his hands linger there. He looks up. Ryan's frowning.

"So, um. You know how I kissed you last night?"

Ryan nods.

"Well, it turns out I'm a little late to this party, but I'd really like to do it again. Properly, this time."

Ryan freezes. "What?"

"Can I kiss you, Ryan?"

"Why?" It's said so softly Jesse's lip reading more than hearing the word come out of Ryan's mouth.

Uncertainty creeps into Jesse's chest and makes him drop his hands to his knees. Ryan said in love—but maybe he didn't mean in love, like, wanting to kiss in love? He bites his lip, not sure how to respond. "Uh. Because you're really hot? But we don't have to." As long as Ryan doesn't leave, Jesse thinks they can figure this out.

Ryan stands up, and Jesse's hope ebbs. "I can't—this is why—" He sighs, sounding exasperated. "No, Jesse."

No. Well. Okay then. Jesse stands up, too, shoving his hands in his jean pockets so he won't be tempted to touch Ryan again. "Okay, that's fine. No kissing. What-ever you want, Ryan."

Ryan laughs without humor. "We're really messed up, you know? Can you untangle yourself from what you think I want for five seconds? I just told you I'm in love with you and your reaction was to have a panic attack and then try to kiss me. That's why I better get a flight home. There's probably one out of Boston tonight." Ryan pulls out his phone, as if he can't wait to get as far away from Jesse as possible.

"But I don't want you to leave," Jesse says, knowing he sounds like a whiny toddler.

"Sorry, Jess. Sometimes you don't get what you want," Ryan says. Then he goes into his bedroom and shuts the door.

THIRTEEN

THERE'S no red eye to Nashville, but Ryan grabs a ticket on the first flight out tomorrow. That'll give him time to pack and find a ride to Boston. He probably needs to talk to Cameron, too. And Hank. He opens his closet door and looks at the few things hanging inside. His mind is blank, his heart feels frozen. If he can just make it back home without breaking down, he'll be doing okay.

He has a detached, floating kind of sensation. It sort of reminds him of when he joined the Peace Corps. The decision is made—he doesn't have to worry about whether or not it's the right one.

He fills his bag with clothes, realizes he left his notebook and his phone charger in the living room. He only hesitates a minute before opening the door to the common area. He'd expected Jesse to have moved but he's still there, as if Ryan's last words had turned him to stone.

He keeps his head down and grabs his notebook, his guitar, the charger, and oh, his water bottle and—

"Ryan."

He hums noncommittally, arms full. Did he have this much stuff when he left Nashville for the tour?

"I know I messed up. Again." Jesse's voice sounds choked. "And I'm sorry."

Ryan falters. He's always been a sucker for Jesse, always wanting to give him what he wants. If he's hurting, Ryan wants to help make him feel better. Then he remembers that they're dealing with something more serious than a bad review or an uncooperative melody.

"I just—please tell me we're going to be okay," Jesse says.

Ryan doesn't know how to promise that when everything seems so upside down. But as much as it hurts to be around Jesse right now, it would hurt more to keep away from him forever. He has to believe they'll find a way back to some kind of friendship.

He forces himself to look at Jesse. His face is an odd collection of angles and slopes, sharp edges and soft curves. Ryan knows every plane of Jesse's face better than he knows his own. He still remembers opening his eyes after the explosion, his entire field of vision filled by Jesse. He remembers thinking that if he was about to die, there were a lot worse final things to see than a good-looking guy gazing down on him with concern and relief.

He didn't die that day. He was reborn when Jesse wormed his way into his life. Ryan doesn't know how to be a whole person apart from Jesse. Even if Jesse loved him back the way Ryan so desperately loves him, maybe it wouldn't be a good idea to get involved when so much of Ryan's identity has been wrapped up in Jesse for so long.

He takes a deep breath. Jesse looks like he's holding his. "I want us to be okay. That's all I can promise, Jess." He holds Jesse's gaze for another beat, then turns around and goes back to his room.

The next time he comes out, Jesse is gone.

JESSE TRUDGES slowly down the main path with no real aim in mind. He'd gone up in the woods earlier and it hadn't helped much, either. He can't remember being this tangled up since the days before he joined the Corps, when he didn't know how to make his music career happen and he didn't know if he was cut out to do anything else. The Peace Corps had given him such lovely clarity—just do the thing right in front of him, help the most people he could. Spend his nights writing lyrics for some unknowable fantasy future.

Well, Ryan's right—he's living the future he always dreamed of. He has a music career. People all over the country sing along to lyrics that he wrote when they hear his songs on the radio.

But none of it means anything if Ryan isn't in his life.

He's cold from the tip of his nose to the bones inside his stupid body. Ryan's leaving. Because Jesse's been too unaware to see what his best friend has been dealing with for a while, it sounds like. And whatever Jesse tries to do to make it better seems to blow up in his face.

Bad choice of words.

He rubs the scar on the back of his arm through his jacket.

The lodge is lit up like a goddamn postcard advertising a cheerful winter getaway. Except there's no snow.

No snow, because Jesse's such a loser he brought his best friend to a place with no snow to get into the mood to do a stupid Christmas album.

He almost turns away from the lodge out of spite, but he really has no place else to go. The keys to the SUV are back in the cabin. Maybe Ryan will take the car to get to the airport. Thinking about Ryan flying back to Tennessee alone leaves him even colder than before. He pushes through the lodge's main doors and the shock of heated air almost sends him outside again. He doesn't deserve to be warm and comfy, not when his heart is iced over in terror that he might never see Ryan again.

He remembers Emma telling him they host a wine and cheese hour in the room with the fireplace in the late afternoon, but he and Ryan haven't checked it out yet. He glances down the hallway that leads to Hank's quarters, but he can't go down there. A thought occurs to him —does Hank know about Ryan's feelings? Is that what all those texts have been about?

He feels slightly dizzy as he considers the implications once again. Ryan *loves* him. Or he did, before Jesse proved himself an enormous fool. The idea that Ryan could have been feeling this way for months and Jesse had no idea—he doesn't know what to do with that. He feels like a bad friend, that Ryan had to live with this on his own. He knows Ryan isn't the most forthcoming about his feelings all the time, but still. Then again, he knew *something* was wrong, didn't he? He'd noticed the light going out of Ryan's eyes, the way he'd lost interest in dating. He'd chalked it up to missing Cameron, not developing feelings for Jesse himself. How was he supposed to know if Ryan didn't tell him?

And why is Ryan jumping to the conclusion that Jesse doesn't feel the same way? Why is he pushing him away at the first chance the two of them have to explore this new—

Jesse claps himself on the forehead. These aren't new feelings for Ryan. He's been letting this fester for god knows how long. Jesse's the one who only just woke up and smelled the Ryan.

Only, that's not really true, either. Jesse forces himself to be excruciatingly honest with himself. He's had opportunities to settle down with a long-term girl-friend or boyfriend a few times over the past six years. But he's always told himself that he's better off single and free to hook up with whoever, whenever. But he didn't always feel that way. Before he left for the Corps, he always assumed he'd end up in a monogamous relation-ship once he met the right person. That he'd happily settle down like his parents, the most boringly happy couple he knows. It was only once he met Ryan that keeping himself unattached seemed like the right thing to do. Being available for Ryan, as a friend and as a creative partner, was more satisfying than any of the one night stands he's had over the past six years.

Oh shit. Has he accidentally been saving himself for

Ryan? Is this what he wanted all along—to be Ryan's in all ways, just as he wants Ryan to be his?

If that's true, then he's made an even bigger fool of himself than he thought. Because Ryan laid it all out there, laid his love out there. And Jesse tried to kiss him. Because he's *hot*.

He looks toward the hall that leads to the great room. He can hear music and talking. He shouldn't be with people right now, his stupid might rub off on them, but he can't go back to the cabin. Ryan made it clear he needs space. If Jesse goes there and tries to tell him that he—that he—

Jesse can't even say it in his own head. Because it's too huge. It's too—

Oh, who is he kidding? He's in love with Ryan Winslow and he sort of has been since the day Ryan blinked his big blue eyes at him half a world away. Or maybe even before that, since the first time Jesse heard his smooth twang singing "Cowboy Livin'" on the radio a million years ago. Maybe Jesse's been in love with Ryan since before he can even remember, since he was some other person in some other life.

Suddenly, his fear drops away. He may be a giant doofus, but he's also stubborn. And persuasive. He can convince Ryan that he loves him back, he's certain of it. He's just not sure how. Yet.

Food might help him think. He walks slowly to the great room, takes in the clusters of guests around the circular fireplace. Emma's at the bar in the corner, chatting with Cameron.

He almost forgot about that little wrinkle. He sidles up to them, not sure how he'll be received.

"Hey, Jesse," Emma greets him warmly. Clearly, she's not in the loop about what an ass he's been.

"Hi, Emma. Cameron." He nods at the older man tightly. "Can we talk for a minute?"

Cameron narrows his eyes at him, then picks up a long-necked beer. "Yeah, I think we should," he says. "If you'll excuse us, Miss Emma." He gives Emma a courtly little bow and she laughs.

"You two know each other?" Jesse asks. There's a cheese board on the bar and he grabs a small plate and starts filling it.

"I worked here in high school, remember?" Cameron says. "Haven't been back in a while, but the place looks really great."

"We've worked hard on it." Emma glows with pride. "Though we have a lot more planned."

"We?" Cameron asks.

"Me and Hank. He moved back here a few years ago," she explains.

"H-Hank lives here now?" Cameron asks.

Jesse looks up from his plate to see a funny expression cross Cameron's face.

"Yeah. He'll be around later. I'm sure he'll want to see you," she says.

"He probably doesn't even remember me," Cameron says, a definite blush stealing over his cheeks. "I was just another summer worker."

"Yeah, but Hank was home that summer from school. I remember," Emma says, "you always played the piano when you were on break." She nods to the corner, where a baby grand is partially hidden by the Christmas tree. "Hank loved it. He was always humming the tunes you played."

Cameron's blush gets darker, and Jesse fights a smile. He and Emma exchange a glance and his matchmaker gene is activated in a big way. But he's more concerned with his own love life than with Cameron's at the moment. He swallows a Vermont cheddar-topped cracker and waves at Emma. "We'll be back in a second," he says, steering Cameron to a quiet corner.

"So, uh," Jesse starts eloquently, before he realizes he has no idea what he should say. Cameron is Ryan's ex-boyfriend. No matter how friendly the terms of the breakup, Cameron probably doesn't want to give Jesse advice on how to win Ryan's heart. "Um."

"Look, man," Cameron says when it's clear Jesse's not going to be uttering more than a syllable at a time, "it's nice to see you two, but I don't really want to get in the middle of whatever you have going on."

"We don't have anything going on," Jesse says automatically, giving the response he would give to the press or to inquisitive fans. Then his shoulders slump. "Okay. I really messed up. Ryan says he's going back to Nashville tomorrow. He says he can't," he swallows hard against the lump in his throat, "be around me right now."

Cameron frowns. "That's not like Ryan. I mean, you two are joined at the hip."

"Yeah. Well. I screwed up and he needs space, but I can't fix it if he goes away."

"What did you do?" Cameron asks.

Jesse hesitates. If he tells Cameron they came here because Jesse wanted to throw Ryan and Cameron back together romantically, he'll have to tell him why that plan flamed out so spectacularly, and that's not exactly his information to share. Plus, it's not like Cameron wants to know his ex is in love with someone else.

Cameron sighs. "I can guess."

Or maybe he already knows.

Cameron slowly turns the bottle in his hands. "What Ryan and I had wasn't forever, and I was okay with that. But I kind of felt sorry for you both, because you had this precious thing and didn't seem to realize it. I'm sorry if you're hurting, if Ryan's hurting. But if the two of you are finally figuring out what you have, then a little hurt is worth it. You're the luckiest bastards I know. Disgustingly handsome. Talented as fuck. And you live and breathe each other like it's the most normal thing in the world. Everyone's jealous of that, and you don't even know how good you have it." Cameron could sound bitter, but he doesn't. He sounds like a guy who wants what Jesse was too stupid to notice he already had.

"I always thought he'd never see me like that," Jesse says quietly, "so I didn't let myself—and now he thinks it's just physical for me and he's going to leave."

"You can stop him," Cameron says. "You only have to bat your big pretty eyes at him, and he'll do anything you say, anyway." He only sounds mildly disgruntled.

Jesse's worried he's run out of his lifetime allotment of playing the "I saved your life" card.

But maybe the universe is on his side. A second later,

Hank runs into the great room in a parka and hat. "Ems! Look," he says, pointing to the big picture window.

Emma and everyone else in the place look outside. Big, fat snowflakes drift to the ground and it's cold enough that they're already starting to accumulate.

"Snow!" Emma cries.

"Just heard the updated forecast," Hank says, striding over to the bar. "It's supposed to last all night and into the morning. Eight inches, at least, with more coming."

"Snow. That's a sight for sore eyes," Cameron says, grinning. Jesse can't help noticing Cameron is looking more at Hank than outside.

Snow means Ryan might not be able to get out of Columbia. Snow means Jesse might get a second chance.

FOURTEEN

THINGS HAPPEN QUICKLY AFTER THAT. Emma calls Hank over and asks him to watch the bar so she can make sure the walkways are sanded and the snow shovels are ready. Hank takes one look at Jesse and frowns.

"What happened?" Hank asks as he peels off his hat and coat.

Part of Jesse wants to deflect and stall, but he's done hiding from his feelings. "I have a problem. I need your help. Well, Ryan needs your help. Okay, we both do."

"Spit it out, Jesse."

"Ryan's leaving, tonight, I think. We talked and... some things came to light."

"Things?" Hank says heavily. "You boys finally told each other?"

Jesse represses a flare of anger. If everyone and their brother knows Ryan has—had—*has* feelings for Jesse, and if he's been just as transparent, why hasn't anyone done him a solid and actually let him in on it? "Jesus, does everyone know?"

Hank ignores him. "What's the problem and why is Ryan leaving? Unless you—"

"Yeah. Okay. I didn't exactly respond the way I should have. But I can fix it."

"You better," Hank says sternly. "I've never met two people more meant for each other and more clueless about it."

Hank's words warm Jesse even as he cringes under Hank's critical eye. He and Ryan are meant for each other. If nothing else, he believes that with his whole heart. He straightens his spine. "I'm going to do better."

"See that you do," Hank says. He looks to Cameron, who's been standing a foot behind Jesse for this entire painful exchange. "Hi," he says, his tone softening. "I'm Hank Moore."

"I know," Cameron says.

Jesse shifts so Cameron can come stand next to him and allows himself to enjoy the return of Cameron's blush.

"I'm Cameron Keane. You wouldn't remember, but I spent a summer working here at the lodge ages ago."

Hank's eyes widen a little and he takes Cameron in again, sweeping his gaze across him from head to foot and back again. "Cameron? The kid who'd sneak off to play that old piano every chance he got?"

"That would be me."

"Wow, it's been, what—fifteen years?"

"Closer to twenty," Cameron says with a bashful smile.

"There's something in the air around here," Hank

says. "It's a week for reunions. I take it you know Jesse here?"

"Oh yeah." Cameron chuckles. "I know Jesse. Told him about this place, actually. Ryan and I went out for a while. But how do you know each other?"

"We were in the Peace Corps together. Did two years in Africa with Jesse, a few months with Ryan," Hank says. "Small world."

"This is wild—who would have thought someone from my tiny hometown would have ended up in the Peace Corp with two of my buddies? And now you're back home. Funny how the more things change, the more they stay the same."

Hank smiles slowly and Jesse swears he winks. "Looks like you grew up good, though."

Jesse stifles a grin as Cameron turns bright red. He's happy if the sparks he senses between Cameron and Hank lead to something great for them, but he's on the clock. "Cameron just came back from touring, and I'm sure he'd love to play for you, but—"

Hank breaks in with an impressed whistle. "I'm surrounded by talent," he says. "And I definitely would love to hear you play."

Jesse claps his hands briskly. "Great! So you two will do that but first I need you to do something for me. Hank—can you text Ryan and make sure he doesn't get on the road tonight? It's too dangerous with the snow."

Hank's thick eyebrows push together, and he nods. "I wouldn't want anybody on the road during this storm."

"Cameron, do you have a guitar I can borrow?"

"What's wrong with yours?"

"I'm not ready to see Ryan yet. Please, can I borrow yours?"

"I've got one upstairs," Cameron says grudgingly. "What's all this about?"

"Just keep Ryan on the property. Cameron, maybe you can invite him for dinner here at the lodge. I need to work on something, and I can't let him go back to Nashville without telling him how I feel. If he still wants to leave after that, well, that's up to him."

"You can use my room upstairs," Cameron says, handing over his key.

"Thank you so much, really. I know I've been an unforgivable jackass, but I promise I—"

"Just go!" Cameron pushes his shoulder and Hank makes a shooing motion with his hands.

"All right. Thanks, guys," he says, walking backwards toward the lobby.

Hank slides over to Cameron. "I'll call Ryan. Can you hang out for a while just in case? These two need all the help they can get."

Jesse waits until he sees the pleased smile flit across Cameron's face before he turns around and runs for the stairs. He's not going to waste this opportunity. He has so many thoughts swirling around in his oversized head and he needs to get them down on paper and make some sense of them. It's the only thing he can think of that will show Ryan just how much Jesse needs him. Just how much he wants him. Just how much he loves him.

Just please let it not be too late.

RYAN'S PHONE rings just as he's about to book a ride to the airport. It'll cost more than his plane ticket, but he's desperate.

"Hey, Hank," he says wearily. The numbness after his talk with Jesse is wearing off, being replaced by a soreness under his breastbone that he keeps touching. It's as if his heartache is a tangible thing, something he wants to rub away, or take something to dull. But there's no cure for what ails him, except maybe time and space, both of which he's reluctantly forcing upon himself.

"Ryan, where are you?" Hank sounds worried.

"In the cabin, why?"

"Haven't you noticed? It's snowing."

"Seriously?" The days are short this time of year, and he'd drawn the blinds in the cabin's main room when the sun started going down. Now he pushes one up and squints against the glare on the glass to see a thin blanket of white covering everything outside. His initial instinct is to call for Jesse to come see. Jesse loves snow even more than Ryan. He's an avid snowboarder and never passes up a chance to fling a snowball in Ryan's general vicinity. But Jesse's not here.

"So stay there, understand?" Hank's being strangely insistent but Ryan brushes it off.

"Actually, I was going to call you. I'm heading home tomorrow. Got a ticket on a flight out of Boston. Was going to leave before dawn, but I wanted to say goodbye first."

"I don't think that's a good idea. We might get a foot overnight. No telling what the roads are going to be like pretty soon. You better stay put."

Ryan imagines being trapped inside the cabin with Jesse while snow piles up outside. A day ago he might have thought that scenario could lead to their relationship changing for the better, or at least be a fertile time to work on their album. But at the moment it sounds like torture. He can't look at Jesse and see the pity and the pain and all the other emotions that Ryan's inflicted on him by being so stupid as to fall in love with his best friend. "No, I can't do that."

"I hate to tell you, but the weather isn't going to cooperate. You can get a flight in a day or two when things clear up."

"Then I'll go now. The roads can't be that bad yet." He spots the rental car keys on the kitchen table. Jesse must have gone for another walk.

"What? No, Ryan—"

"Wait, Jesse's with you, isn't he? He's at the lodge?"

"Uh. He's at the lodge, but he's not with me," Hank says, sounding distracted. It almost sounds like there's another voice whispering just out of discernible range on the phone. Is Hank lying? Is Jesse telling him what to say?

Ryan scoops the keys up without a second thought. "Tell Jesse I'm taking the SUV. I'll pay him back later. Bye, Hank." He hangs up, feeling only mildly guilty.

Quickly, he grabs his suitcase and his guitar case, shuts the lights off in the cabin, puts on his coat and hat. He leaves his cabin key inside and shuts the door behind him. Two minutes later he's cleared the layer of snowfall from the SUV's windshield and is steering it down the path, past the lodge entrance and onto the road. His phone's been buzzing nonstop, but he doesn't answer. Let Jesse not get what he wants for a change.

He's two miles down the road before he realizes he's gripping the steering wheel so tight he can feel the imprint of the leather stitching on his palms. He relaxes his hold. The roads aren't too bad. The snow's falling harder than he expected, and he didn't think to check the SUV's tires before he got in the vehicle, but it's a luxury rental, they're probably fine. He can outrun this storm, get to Boston, sit up in the airport all night for all he cares.

He's almost out of Columbia, heading for the road that'll take him to the Interstate, when the snow starts coming down even harder. He flips the wipers on full blast, but visibility isn't good. In fact, it's downright shitty. His high beams seem to only illuminate a few feet in front of him. He eases his foot off the gas, but his lower speed doesn't help him as he finds himself crossing a bridge and his tires start slipping. He has a second to remember that bridges freeze before roads and then the SUV slides into the railing with an ominous crunching shudder.

FIFTEEN

JESSE HUMS, strums, and then hums again. He's almost got it. He's always been a fast writer—first drafts come easily to him. The hard work comes later, writing the music, refining the song into something unique and essential. Tonight, he has so many feelings coursing through him the words have been bubbling up faster than he can get them down on paper, but the music is coming fast, too, a simple tune that he's pouring his entire soul into.

Ryan wrote him a song, and Jesse's returning the favor. It's the only way he can think of to break through this impasse and show Ryan how he feels. He has to speak Ryan's language, which means music.

He runs through the fingering on his borrowed guitar. Should he repeat the last verse? He frowns, sings the last few lines under his breath. He's written in high-pressure situations before, but never like this. It feels like his entire future rests on getting these words just right. At the same time, he's certain he can get through to

Ryan. Hank's right—they are meant to be together. Jesse knows that now. He wishes he hadn't spent so many years telling himself he couldn't—shouldn't—want Ryan that way. But they have their entire lives stretching ahead of them. He can't help smiling when he thinks of all the amazing things they have to look forward to. He can't wait to take Ryan out on their first proper date. He wants to spoil him, to make him never regret giving Jesse a chance.

He knows he's assuming awful lot, and he wouldn't blame Ryan for deciding Jesse's just not worth the trouble, but he knows Ryan and his big heart. Whether Jesse deserves a second chance or not, Ryan's always been a soft touch. Jesse resolves to earn Ryan's grace from now until the end of time.

He's running through the beginning of the song again when someone starts hammering on the door to Cameron's room. What the hell? Jesse gets up—the door's rattling on its hinges with the force of the blows when he opens it to find Cameron on the other side, fist raised as if to knock again.

"Jesse, Jesus, we've been calling you," Cameron says, straining to catch his breath.

"Why? What's wrong?" Jesse feels cold and he doesn't know why.

"It's Ryan. He left the lodge in your car, and we were trying to decide if we should go after him, but then Hank got a call from emergency services that there'd been an accident. He's going to open up the clinic."

Jesse can't comprehend what Cameron is telling

him. "An accident—Ryan? How bad—" He can't even finish that sentence in his head.

"I don't know. Hank thought you'd want to come to the clinic, but you weren't answering."

"I put my phone on silent so I could concentrate. Has he left yet?" Jesse reaches back to grab his jacket from the bed, leaving behind everything else.

"I don't know. You might be able to catch him."

Jesse runs, tearing down the staircase to the lobby in time to see Hank's truck pulling away from the entrance. He bursts out of the door, yelling at the top of his lungs. He races through the snow, which is pouring from the sky like feathers from a torn pillow, certain Hank's not going to stop. But then his brake lights go on, and the pickup slows. Jesse's eternally grateful he's still wearing his boots from his walk in the woods earlier that day. He snaps open the door and hauls himself into the cab, taking in Hank's worried posture. It's only when Hank pulls carefully onto the road that he realizes he's still clutching his jacket. He puts in on mechanically.

"Buckle up," Hank says gruffly.

Jesse does as he's told, then gets his phone out of his jacket pocket. He stares at the screen while Hank explains he doesn't know much more than there was a single car accident on Echo Bridge and the cops are bringing the driver to the clinic to get checked out. He's listening to Hank, but his eyes are on his notifications. Three calls from Cameron, one from an unknown number that must be Hank's. And one from Ryan. When had Ryan called him? Before he left? After his accident? Ryan had needed Jesse and Jesse hadn't been there for him.

"Can you go any faster?" It's a childish question. He's lucky to be tagging along at all.

But Hank answers in a soft voice. "I'm going as fast as I can. It's not far, but the roads haven't been plowed."

"Should I call him?" Jesse has never needed to hear someone's voice as much as he needs to hear Ryan's right now.

"You can try, but we'll be there in a minute anyway."

Jesse punches the call button before Hank finishes talking. It takes a while for the connection to go through but eventually the phone starts to ring. Hank turns onto Main Street, and Jesse spots the forest green police cruiser parked in front of the squat clinic building. As they approach and pull in next to the cruiser, Jesse can see Ryan's silhouette in the back of the car and he just about passes out from relief. Ryan's sitting up. He's not answering his phone, but that doesn't matter now. Jesse hops out the second Hank puts the truck into park.

"Ryan!" He waves at the window, not caring if he looks like an idiot in front of Hank or the two uniformed police officers sitting in the front seat. Ryan turns his head at the sound of Jesse's voice. For a moment Jesse flashes back to the first time he was on the outside looking at Ryan through a car window and his heart misses a beat in fear. Ryan holds his gaze, his expression unreadable, but he's awake and alert. This isn't six years ago. Jesse breathes out heavily.

The driver's door opens, and a slightly built woman gets out. "You're not Dr. Moore," she observes.

"I'm Jesse Arlyn," he says, jerking his head to the side. "Hank's right here."

"Hey, Letty," Hank says, unlocking the front door of the clinic with a set of jangling keys. "Find me a customer?"

"Yeah, an out-of-towner who doesn't know how to drive in snow," the officer—Letty—says dispassionately as she opens the rear door. "But he'll live."

"Ryan, are you okay? What happened? Are you hurt? Talk to me." Jesse can't help the flood of words as Ryan gingerly gets out of the car, holding his right arm.

"I'm okay," Ryan says. "The rental's pretty banged up, though. Did you get the extra insurance?"

Jesse is helpless against the tears that fill his eyes. "Please don't joke right now, Jesus." He hovers by Ryan's side as they walk the ten feet to the clinic entrance through the slippery snow. Ryan's sneakers look soaked through, and his jeans are wet in patches, too. "You're all wet. You must be freezing."

"You all set here?" Letty asks.

Hank nods. "I've got him. You guys stay safe out there tonight," he says, ushering Ryan and Jesse into the warm clinic. They pass a small waiting area with a desk, then Hank leads them through to an exam room. He washes his hands at the sink while he asks Ryan what hurts.

"Just my elbow, I think," Ryan says as he sits down on the exam table. "I'm really fine. I didn't even get hurt in the crash. I got out of the car and then fell on my ass—actually, on my elbow."

Jesse jumps in. "But how did the car crash? Where? Why were you even on the road?"

Hank steps right up to his face and all Jesse can see are Hank's steely brown eyes. "Jesse Arlyn, you have two choices. You can sit down in that chair and keep your mouth shut or you can go wait outside."

Jesse tries to peer around Hank to check in with Ryan, but Hank doesn't budge. He opens his mouth and Hank's glare hardens. He slowly closes his mouth, turns around, and drops into the hard plastic chair in the corner. As Hank turns his attention away, Jesse tries to catch Ryan's gaze with his own, but Ryan isn't looking at him.

"Let's see," Hank says. Ryan tries to remove his jacket, but the motion seems to bother his elbow. Hank helps him peel off his outer layer, then the thick flannel shirt underneath, then roll up the sleeve of his green long-sleeved tee. He assesses Ryan's arm and elbow joint with long, capable fingers.

Jesse wriggles in his seat, trying to quell the spike of jealousy at Hank touching Ryan. He knows the touch is clinical, that he needs to determine the damage. He was an EMT himself a lifetime ago. He knows how it works. But his own fingers itch with the need to touch Ryan, to reassure himself his friend is in one piece.

When Ryan attempts to extend his arm, he winces in pain.

"It might be broken," Hank says. "We won't be certain until you get an X-ray. We don't have those facilities here. But even if it's just a bad bruise and sprain, the treatment is basically the same. I'm going to wrap it, give you a sling. You're going to ice it and elevate it and take pain meds as needed."

"Damn," Ryan says ruefully. "I need this arm to play."

Jesse hadn't realized that an immobile right arm means Ryan won't be able to pick up a guitar for a while.

"It'll heal up in a few weeks," Hank says in his calm doctor's tone, "if you take care of it properly. We'll know a bit more after the scan. For now, let's get some ice on there. I'm going to grab a few things and be right back. You." He points at Jesse. "Chill." Then he leaves, the door standing open.

Jesse presses his lips together and sucks the seam between his teeth to keep himself from talking.

"I know the truly herculean effort you are making," Ryan says, looking at his feet instead of at Jesse, "and I promise I'll explain what happened. You can yell at me all you want later." He glances up, his eyes aqua under the fluorescent lights. "But right now, can I just get a hug?"

Jesse pushes to his feet, crosses the little room, and puts his arms around Ryan, being extremely careful of Ryan's injured elbow. He tucks his chin onto Ryan's shoulder, folds his body as close as he can with the exam table exaggerating their height imbalance. He takes a deep breath, Ryan smelling reassuringly like himself. He feels the moment Ryan relaxes into the hug, his shoulders dropping, his uninjured arm curving around Jesse's side. They've hugged lots of times, one-armed bro-hugs and quick squeezes and jocular pats on the back. Jesse's never sunk into Ryan's space and stayed there. He's never let himself turn his face toward Ryan's neck and let his nose graze Ryan's skin. He wants to press a kiss to that skin, over Ryan's pulse, but Ryan only said he wanted a hug. Jesse's going to do a better job of listening.

"I'm really glad you're here," Ryan says, his voice gravelly. "I thought I was seeing things when you got out of Hank's truck."

"I'm here," Jesse whispers. "I'll always be here."

Ryan shifts and Jesse looks up just as Hank walks back into the room his hands full of supplies. He lets go of Ryan reluctantly, squeezes his shoulder briefly, then sits in his chair again before Hank can lecture him.

Ryan's cheeks have more color now. Hank wraps his elbow and arm, applies ice, and shows him how to use the sling.

"I'll tell you where you can make an appointment to get an X-ray, and I'll check on your arm tomorrow."

"Thanks, Hank. I'm sorry about this. You tried to tell me not to go and I didn't listen."

"Hey, I'm not mad. I'm just glad you're okay." Hank glances between them. "Though if I never had to patch up either of you knuckleheads again, I'd be a happy man."

"Me too," Ryan says on a sigh. "So, are we stuck here?"

"Actually, I saw them plowing Main Street. I'll call Emma and see if the road up to the lodge has been cleared yet and then we can go back. Locals aren't dumb enough to go out in this weather, so hopefully my phone won't be ringing again tonight."

While Hank calls Emma, Jesse helps Ryan put his

flannel and jacket on his non-injured side and tuck them around his immobilized arm as best he can. Ryan looks as if he wants to say something, but when Jesse raises an eyebrow in question, he shakes his head. Later.

The roads are better since the plow and the sander came through, and they pile into Hank's truck for the short drive to the lodge. When they get there, Jesse realizes they all missed dinner.

Hank parks and they enter through the front. "Emma said she left a tray behind the bar. You two go ahead. I'm still on call, so I'll check in with you tomorrow. Don't be a hero about the pain, Ryan. Take something when you need to."

"Yes, sir," Ryan says. He has shadows under his eyes and Jesse wonders if they should skip dinner and go straight to the cabin and turn in. But pain meds will go down better with food, so he gives Hank a short hug, tells him a heartfelt thank you, and they make their way to the great room.

There's a fire in the fire pit, and a cluster of people playing a board game on one of the breakfast tables. Jesse steers Ryan to a comfortable looking chair near the fire, then goes to the bar and finds a tray of sandwiches. He liberates a few bottles of water from the bar's under-counter mini fridge. They eat in silence, and when Ryan's put away half a roast beef sandwich, a bottle of water, and three ibuprofen, Jesse allows himself to relax. The fire is throwing off a lot of heat and his lids are starting to droop after the emotional turmoil of the day, with its nearly catastrophic ending. Ryan looks ready to lean back in his chair and fall asleep.

"You must be tired," Jesse says. "Let's go back to the cabin. My bathroom has that big soaking tub. You can use it, take a long bath."

"I am tired. And a bath sounds good. But don't you want to talk?"

He wants to say yes, to tell Ryan what he realized, to beg him for another chance to respond to the earth-shattering news that Ryan's in love with him, properly this time. But it'll keep. They're together, and Ryan's safe, and the snow's still falling. His feelings aren't going away.

"Tomorrow."

SIXTEEN

JESSE'S so tired by the time he falls into bed he sleeps like the dead for eight hours and wakes up to thin gray light coming through the edges of the blinds in his room. The cabin feels chilly, and he throws on a sweater and heavy socks before shuffling out to see if he can get something resembling coffee to come out of the machine in the kitchenette. He stops at the sight of Ryan asleep on the too-short couch, his legs curled up toward his belly, lying on his non-injured side. The blanket from his bedroom is clenched around him and there's a groove between his eyebrows.

Ryan's in pain.

Quietly, Jesse moves through the cabin, fills a glass with water, drinks half of it while looking in their fridge. He sets the glass down and wrinkles his nose at the leftovers from taco night. He checks the time. They've started serving breakfast in the lodge. He'll get dressed and get food and real coffee and when he gets back he'll make Ryan take more pain relievers. But when he turns to go back to his room, Ryan's sitting up on the couch, his hair sticking up every which way.

Jesse moves to Ryan's side, crouching on the floor. He gets a buzzy feeling in his stomach seeing Ryan wear his Titans T-shirt and a pair of his sweats. Ryan's stuff got left behind in last night's commotion.

"Hey." Ryan's voice is scratchy, and he has purple smudges under his eyes as if he hasn't slept at all.

"Hi." As ever, Jesse's brain is full of questions, but he sticks to the most important ones. "How's your arm? Time to ice it more?"

"It hurts a little," Ryan admits. "Ice would be good."

Jesse retrieves an extra cold pack from the freezer box and brings it to Ryan. "I'm going to get us some breakfast, then you can take something."

Ryan lets out a loud yawn in response.

"Why aren't you in bed?" Jesse's about to order him back to his bedroom, but he tells himself to wait for Ryan's answer. As much as he wants to bully Ryan back to good health, he has to do better, has to really listen to his friend.

"I fell asleep okay, but then—" Ryan fiddles with the ice pack, holding it to his elbow gingerly.

Jesse waits. Is his bed uncomfortable? Do they need to get him more pillows?

"I had, um, a nightmare. I was in the car, but not the car last night. The one in—I was trapped inside, and there was fire all around, and I could see you through the window, but I couldn't get out. Couldn't get to you. And you couldn't get to me. I woke up...and I came out here. Fell back asleep eventually."

"Oh." Ryan's nightmare sounds eerily similar to the ones he has from time to time. He shivers. "You should have woken me up."

"I thought about it, but I didn't want to bother you."

"Next time, wake me up. Okay?"

Ryan looks up, his eyes wide as if he wasn't expecting that. He cocks his head to the side. "What's up with you?"

"What do you mean?"

"You're being weird."

Jesse's first instinct is to deflect, but he realizes the time for that is over. Before, he always had to obscure his care for and attention to Ryan with friendly bonhomie or ribbing, or melodramatically use his own injury from all those years ago to disguise how deep his regard for Ryan's well-being runs. He's never simply been able to be...soft with Ryan. To treat him like the precious person he is without a layer of artificial posturing in the way.

He smiles. "No, I'm good. Really good." He gets to his feet. "But I'll be even better after breakfast. Why don't I get you set up in bed, and I'll go to the lodge for provisions. Hey, I wonder how much snow we got?" He crosses to the big window and draws the blinds. The world outside has been completely transformed with a blanket—no, more like a big fluffy comforter—of snow. He turns to Ryan excitedly. "Hey, looks like maybe a foot. And it's still coming down."

Ryan doesn't seem appropriately excited. He looks out the window, then away.

"What's wrong? You were the one who wanted snow."

"It's not that. Um. Let me put on my clothes and I'll come with you." Ryan stands up and walks stiffly toward his room.

"Ryan, no, seriously. Stay here and I'll be right back—"

"I want to come with you," Ryan says stubbornly.

"We don't know what the path is like. It could be slippery. You don't want to fall again."

"I only fell yesterday because—" Ryan bites his lip.

Jesse tells himself sternly not to be distracted by incidentally sexy lip biting. "Because why?"

"I told you I had a nightmare. But last night, when the SUV hit the bridge guard rail. I kind of—had a flashback—I guess?"

Jesse sucks in a breath at the image of Ryan's car banging against a bridge guard rail. What if the rail had broken? What if he'd gone over the side?

"All of a sudden, I was in the other SUV, just like in my dream. I wasn't hurt—the car wasn't moving very quickly; it didn't even hit my side. But suddenly I felt trapped, and I felt like the car was on fire. I panicked a little. I got my belt off and I got out, and I just felt like I had to get far away. But I didn't make it six steps before I hit the ground. Luckily, I had my phone and I called—" Ryan stops, does the lip biting thing again.

"You called me," Jesse finishes. And he hadn't picked up.

"Yeah. I didn't have any right to, but all I could think in that moment was I wanted you to—well, save me, I guess." Ryan's cheeks take on a pink glow that Jesse will consider adorable later. Now, he's too angry at himself to appreciate Ryan's flush. "But you didn't answer, and I got my shit together and called 911. When the cops arrived, I was more embarrassed than hurt. The car still drove—one of them got it off the bridge and onto the side of the road. And well, you know the rest."

"But why were you driving in the first place? Didn't you realize there was a big storm?"

"I wasn't thinking clearly. I thought I wanted to get away from—" Ryan bites the side of his thumb this time, but the effect is the same.

"You've got to stop cutting off mid-sentence, man," Jesse says, shoving a hand through his hair in exasperation.

"I wanted to get away from you," Ryan mutters.

"Oh." Jesse knows he doesn't have any right to feel hurt, but he still feels the words like a punch in the jaw. "Hey, I get it. I just wish you hadn't been so hasty. And for the record, I'm sorry I didn't answer. I had my phone on silent and I was in the middle of—" This time, it's Jesse's turn to cut off mid-sentence.

Ryan doesn't seem to notice. "It's okay. I can't expect you to bail me out of any crappy situation I get myself into. It was my fault I was out in the storm. My fault I crashed. And I managed to rescue myself. Sort of." He smiles lopsidedly. "We've been living in each other's pockets so long it might take me a minute to figure out how to live on my own. But I'll figure it out."

Jesse's scared to hear the answer, but he has to ask the question. "Is that really what you want?"

"No!" The word booms out of Ryan with the force of a bass drum note. He frowns as if surprised at his own vehemence. "I thought I did. I thought it's what I needed. But it's not what I want. Not ever. How can you ask me that? If you love someone, the last thing you want is to have to start over without them. But that's the only option I'm seeing here, if we're going to keep any pretense of a working relationship. If I want to keep my sanity, or at least my dignity. But no, Jesse," Ryan finishes tiredly, "that's not what I want."

Jesse crosses the room slowly, holding out his hand as if gentling a skittish pony, then dropping it softly on Ryan's uninjured shoulder. "I'm very, very happy to hear you say that," he says. The reality of how close he's come to losing Ryan in every possible way hits him and he blinks against the tears forming in the corners of his eyes. He takes a shaky breath. "I don't want that either. Because I love you."

Ryan jerks away from Jesse's touch, shaking his head. "Don't do that, please don't tell me what you think I want to hear."

"I'm not, I swear on Dolly and Patsy and June, Ryan."

Ryan's eyes go wide at Jesse's invocation of his all-time favorites.

"Look, I know I don't deserve you. I never have. I wormed my way into your life, and you never made me feel like the impostor I am. You deserve—you deserve the whole world. And I'm just a guy who liked to write songs and who blackmailed you into keeping me around. I wasn't allowed to have feelings for you. I wasn't allowed to fall in love with you. But I did it anyway, because I'm a stubborn, thick-headed fool. I do love you. So much. And not just because you're hot."

Jesse holds his breath, not at all certain his impromptu speech will convince Ryan to stay, but he's enough of an optimist to hold out hope.

"You really, um." Ryan's face crumples, and he turns away, covering his mouth with his hand. His shoulders start to shake, and Jesse realizes he's crying.

"Oh, Ryan, darlin', hey, it's okay." Jesse drapes his arm around Ryan, murmuring nonsense that he hopes is soothing, feeling close to tears himself.

He holds Ryan like that for a minute, until Ryan wipes his eyes with the back of his hand and leans back into Jesse's chest. Ryan's breathing evens out but Jesse's worried about his pain level. He still hasn't taken anything for his elbow today.

Before he can change the subject to pain management, Ryan turns around. His beautiful eyes are ringed with red, cheeks shiny wet.

"Sorry," he says, voice thick. "I just—I never thought I'd hear you say that."

"I love you?" Jesse smiles. He likes saying it.

"Yeah, that," Ryan says faintly. "Fuck. I didn't actually die in that car crash, did I? Am I in some kind of afterlife scenario?"

"As nice as it is to hear that me loving you makes you think you're in heaven, can we please stop talking about you dying? It really messes with me, Ryan."

"Yeah, sorry. Too soon. And too soon for that crack about me being hot, Jesse, for the record."

"Noted," Jesse says, but he can't resist adding, "Though you are really hot."

Ryan laughs, and the sound lifts a heavy weight from Jesse's heart. "Yeah? You think so?"

"I know so. And I'm very much looking forward to showing you just how hot I think you are."

"How are you going to do that?" Ryan asks, as if he genuinely has no idea where Jesse's head might be at.

"Well, for starters I'm going to kiss you. Properly this time. The last time was just awful—I can't believe that was our first kiss. Me sloppy and out of line. I'm still so sorry about that." Jesse cringes at the memory.

Ryan takes a step forward, and there wasn't much room between them in the first place. He tilts his head up, his golden lashes darkened by tears, his mouth pink. He puts his free arm around Jesse's waist. "You know what? I think we deserve a do-over. What do you say? Let's have a second first kiss."

"You have the best ideas," Jesse murmurs, and before he can think himself out of it, he dips his head and meets Ryan's lips with his own.

SEVENTEEN

THEIR FIRST FIRST kiss was so brief and had taken him by such surprise, Ryan hadn't been able to catalog anything about it.

Their second first kiss is longer, slower, and infinitely sweeter. Ryan tries to be present for every detail, from the firm pressure of Jesse's softer-than-expected mouth to the sexy little groan he makes when Ryan slips his tongue between the seam of his lips. He opens up readily and the first taste of the inside of Jesse is so perfect that Ryan surges forward, needing more.

Before he realizes it, they've walked themselves to the couch. Jesse sits down heavily. Ryan wastes no time climbing on top of him, straddling him, knees on either side of Jesse's waist. He's fantasized about being in this position so many times, Jesse's long, strong body beneath him, Jesse's enormous hands cradling Ryan's jaw as they stick their tongues down each other's throats. It's every bit as hot as Ryan imagined, gets him turned on just as much as he always suspected it would.

He wants to get closer, to drink Jesse in now that he's miraculously been given access to the precious resource that is Jesse's mouth, but his arm in the sling is getting in the way. He shifts, knocks his elbow against Jesse and it sends a jolt of pain up his arm. A noise of discomfort leaves him before he can call it back.

Jesse stops kissing him immediately at the sound of distress. "Ryan, what's wrong?"

"I'm okay." Ryan doesn't want to stop kissing Jesse. Basically ever.

"No, you're not," Jesse says, physically lifting Ryan back a few inches to give them both room to breathe. The bossy, entitled manhandling should be annoying and it is, but it's also more than a little arousing.

"Where is your ice pack? You need to eat something and then you can take more medicine."

Ryan looks around. The ice pack got lost somewhere between Ryan feeling like his world was crumbling around him and Jesse telling him he's in love. With Ryan. The most wonderful, improbable thing in the world. He still can't quite believe it. If this really is heaven, he doesn't care as long as in this heaven, Jesse loves him back.

"Come on, we'll get breakfast and then you need to rest," Jesse says, shifting Ryan off his lap and onto the couch.

"Killjoy," Ryan mutters. "You know what would really make me feel better? An orgasm. All those endorphins."

He's pleased to see a pink glow steal onto Jesse's cheeks. "Yeah. Well. There will be time for that later."

"Promise?"

"That's a promise I know I can keep," Jesse says. "Now let's get dressed."

HALF AN HOUR later they're in the lodge's great room, basking in the warmth of the fire pit and digging into breakfast. The snow has stopped falling, and the roads have been plowed. Joy told them they got thirteen inches overnight when she brought them coffee. Ryan eats awkwardly with his left hand, but it's not so bad. The food is delicious, the coffee takes the edge off the ache in his arm, and the ibuprofen Jesse thrusts in his face after he's had a few bites of food helps, too.

Even though he's bummed about his elbow and the prospect of not being able to play for a few weeks, it's hard to be in a bad mood when it feels like everything he's ever wanted has been handed to him on a silver platter. Jesse keeps smiling at him, this shy, pleased smile and Ryan can't help but smile back. They probably look disgustingly besotted to anyone within view, but he doesn't care.

He's never felt this way before, like everything is actually going to work out. Jesse's been his grounding force for six years. He had been beginning to think that was a bad thing, keeping Ryan from having to face the world on his own. But now he realizes it's okay. He can make it on his own, but he doesn't have to. He's lucky, he knows that, and he's not going to turn down the best thing that ever happened to him to prove some stupid point to himself.

"What are you thinking about?" Jesse asks as they linger over their coffees.

Ryan takes a moment to answer. "The future, I guess."

"What about it?"

"Just, well, looking forward to it." Ryan feels his cheeks heat and wonders if he can blame the flush on the fire pit.

"Me too," Jesse says, his lips curving up at the edges, his eyes glittering like silver fire.

That's the most mind-blowing part. Not that he and Jesse are actually on the same page about changing their relationship status, or that Jesse's kisses are Ryan's new favorite thing. It's how soft and open Jesse's being with him. It's as if there's been this side of Jesse all along, and Ryan just didn't notice. Jesse's always been careful with him, always acted in his best interests, or tried to. But it's like Ryan was watching Jesse through dark glasses, as if the love and joy inside his friend was too bright for Ryan's eyes, and now the glasses are off, but it turns out Jesse's pure, unadulterated self is actually the perfect frequency for Ryan after all. He wonders if they could have had this a long time ago if only he'd been a little bit braver.

But they're focusing on the future, not the past.

"So, what's next?" He supposes even if they'd like to spend the next week holed up in the cabin, chasing some of those endorphins Ryan is certain will be excellent painkillers, they have other responsibilities.

"Well, first Hank's going to want to look at your elbow. Oh shit, and I completely forgot about Cameron.

He's going to want to know you're okay, too. And I guess we should see about getting the car towed and your stuff back. I'll call the rental company and get that sorted out and—"

"Jess?"

"Yeah?"

"I love how you can populate a to-do list in less than thirty seconds but don't forget to pencil in some time for us."

"Oh. Right." Jesse pushes back from the table. "Well, the sooner we take care of business, the sooner we can go back to the cabin and turn off our phones."

"That's an idea I can definitely get behind. Let's go see if Hank's home."

They walk through the lodge, and for the first time since they got here, Ryan can appreciate the beautiful seasonal decorations, the swaths of greenery, the cheerful red bows. Christmas is just over a week away and he can't believe he and Jesse will be spending it as a couple. He shivers. It almost feels too good to be true.

Emma's at the lobby desk, talking to a couple of young women in puffy winter jackets. When she catches sight of them, she puts up a finger for them to wait. As soon as she sends the other guests on their way, she comes around the desk.

"Ryan, Jesus, are you okay? I heard something about a car wreck?" Emma's face creases with concern.

"I'm really fine," Ryan says, feeling conspicuous. He's never liked being the center of attention, just one reason why his job as a musician has always been an odd fit. As if sensing his discomfort, Jesse angles himself into the space between Emma and Ryan. He brushes his pinkie against the back of Ryan's hand and Ryan fights the smile that wants to spread on his face.

"Well I'm glad you're okay," she says. Is it Ryan's imagination, or does her gaze drop to the vicinity of their almost-touching hands before returning to eye level? If anything, Jesse inches closer.

They may have declared their love for each other, they may have crossed that invisible line from friends to something more, but nothing's really changed. Jesse's still protecting him, just as he always has.

"We're going to get a checkup from Dr. Moore," Jesse says.

"Good, put my brother to work." She smiles and winks at them. "And get better soon."

A minute later, they're knocking on Hank's door. While they wait, muffled voices can be heard inside. They exchange a look, but before Ryan can wonder out loud, Hank opens the door, letting out the smell of coffee and bacon and revealing the owner of the other voice. Cameron is sitting in Hank's living room, his long hair loose, a mug of coffee in his hands.

"Good morning," Jesse says, somehow lacing the two words with extra meaning.

Ryan's a little confused, but he goes inside when Hank ushers them in. "Hey, Hank. Cameron." He hears the question in his voice, but no one rushes to explain.

"How's the elbow?" Hank asks.

"It hurts," Ryan admits. "But not worse than last night. I'm a little stiff all over."

"Makes sense. Rest, ice, compression, elevation. You

should call today and get that X-ray scheduled. Sit down and I'll take a look."

Ryan drops to the sofa, suddenly feeling drained. He really didn't sleep well last night, too caught up in visions of what might have been, anxious that while Jesse didn't seem to mind taking care of him after an accident which was clearly Ryan's own damn fault, that didn't mean Ryan should take advantage of his good nature. But then this morning, everything changed, and that's its own kind of stress, figuring out how to navigate this new world in which he and Jesse are more than friends.

"So, how was your night?" Jesse asks while Hank takes Ryan's sling off and pokes and prods at his elbow. "I take it you both stayed out of the storm?"

"Yeah, well, Hank's a real good host," Cameron says, laughing a little. "I was worried about Ryan and since Jesse didn't respond to any of my texts about how he was doing, I had to ask Hank."

"I'm really sorry about that," Jesse says, looking contrite and sounding serious for the first time since they arrived. "I was a little preoccupied."

Cameron smiles easily. "Like I said, Hank's a good host. He told me Ryan was going to live, and we ended up hunkering down."

"We had a nice time catching up," Hank says, a little smile playing at the corners of his mouth. He glances up from Ryan's elbow, holding his gaze. "You don't mind, do you?"

"Why would I—" Ryan starts, then the penny drops. "Oh." He glances between Hank and Cameron, then over to Jesse, whose eyes are dancing with repressed glee at the prospect of a potential romance. Despite the single embarrassing kiss Ryan would take back if he could, he has no romantic feelings for Hank, and he and Cameron had some good times, but when it ended, they were both happy to stay friends. He doesn't have any claim on them. To the contrary, if they've hit it off, Ryan will be first in line to congratulate them. Or maybe second after Jesse, if the way he's vibrating in his seat is an indication of his feelings on the matter. "Of course not," he says. "I'm a little confused, but I don't mind. Not at all."

Hank straps him back into the sling. "Good. I mean, thanks. And your arm looks pretty fair. Just keep up with the treatment and you'll be back to playing that guitar in no time."

"So, is there a story here?" Ryan asks, nodding at Cameron. "Or is Hank just a magnet for itinerant musicians?"

Cameron pinks up and looks at Hank, who looks back with a secret smile on his face. Oh, for god's sake. He and Jesse seem to have some competition in the sappy looks department.

"Cameron worked here in high school. Hank was home from college. They clearly both had crushes on each other, but I guess it wasn't meant to be until now, because fate brought them together once again at Pine Tree Lodge. You can hire Ryan and me to play at the wedding," Jesse jokes.

"Jesse, shut up," Hank says lightly.

"Am I wrong? There was a lot of unresolved stuff flying between you last night," Jesse says, undeterred.

Cameron rolls his eyes. "You're not wrong, Jesse. You're just an asshole."

Jesse grins and stands up. "I knew it. Come on, Ryan, let's give these two some privacy. You need rest. Let's go to bed and watch *The Big Lebowski.* For some reason, I'm in the mood for it."

Cameron casually shows Jesse his middle finger and Jesse chuckles.

Ryan gets to his feet and lets out a huge yawn. He has a feeling he's not going to make it much past Sam Elliott's intro. He's about to thank Hank, when he sways a little, suddenly lightheaded. Before he can so much as blink, Jesse's there, wrapping one strong arm around his waist, tucking him snugly into his side.

"I got you."

Ryan wants to melt into Jesse's firm, warm body. Without thinking about it, he turns his head to the side and kisses Jesse's shoulder. "I know you do."

He feels Jesse's breath hitch, and it's a second before he realizes what he's done. Was that not okay? He looks up and Jesse's gazing down at him with an expression of such unbearable softness, he feels like melting all over again.

Ryan remembers they have an audience when Hank says, "I feel like I missed something."

Jesse lifts an eyebrow and Ryan nods. It's not like it's not obvious. And if they're really doing this, they're going to have to start telling people. Jesus, the fans are going to flip out when they find out they're fucking in real life. Of course, that's assuming they actually get around to fucking. Then he remembers it's only been hours since fucking was even on the table. He's got to chill. Just because he's wanted this for what feels like a lifetime doesn't mean they need to rush.

"Ryan and I finally figured out we're supposed to be together," Jesse says, his eyes never leaving Ryan's.

"Oh thank the lord," Cameron says dramatically. "Hank and I were worried we'd have to stage an intervention."

"It didn't come to that," Jesse says, finally looking away to their friends. "But I'm awfully glad you two are in our corner. It means a lot."

"Of course," Hank says. "I'm happy for you both. And even happier we're not going to have you two pining all over the place any longer."

Ryan laughs. "There has been a lot of pining, hasn't there? Pining at Pine Tree Lodge. Pining at Pine Tree," he sing-songs. He's feeling a little giddy. The lack of sleep and adrenaline come down might be getting to him.

"Okay, time to go." Jesse laughs and directs Ryan toward the door. "We'll see you guys later."

"Much later," Hank says sternly.

"Much later," Ryan agrees. "Because we're going to be very busy f—" Jesse slams the door shut behind them before Ryan can finish his thought.

"You," Jesse says, once they find themselves alone in the hallway, "are a menace." He punctuates each word with a firm kiss on Ryan's mouth, so Ryan can't even be mad.

"Yeah," Ryan says. "You better take me to bed before I can cause any more trouble."

And Jesse does.

EIGHTEEN

JESSE'S FINALIZING their dinner order on his phone when Ryan stirs beside him. He makes sure the order goes through, then turns off the screen and gazes at Ryan. He's been asleep for almost five hours. When they got back from Hank's, Jesse had bundled Ryan into his bed and he lasted about two minutes into the movie before passing out. Jesse allowed himself the luxury of watching Ryan's face relax into sleep, seeing the groove between his eyebrows disappear, enjoying his perfect mouth drop open slightly. He'd gotten up a minute later, but checked on Ryan every so often, grateful he was able to get some real rest.

Now Ryan blinks his eyes a few times before focusing on Jesse sitting up next to him. "Hi."

"I love you." Jesse frowns. He hadn't meant to say that. But it's so ridiculously true he can't seem to keep it from bursting out.

Ryan contemplates that for a moment. "I believe you do."

A gust of air leaves Jesse's lungs. He needs Ryan to believe that. He surely still has work to do to prove it, but he supposes that's why they make a good match. Ryan believed him when he said they'd be good together in the hospital six years ago. Jesse was right, and Ryan somehow had faith in him.

"Good," Jesse answers, a bit belatedly. He kisses the tip of Ryan's nose, because he's wanted to do that all day, and he can now that Ryan is finally awake. "Dinner's on its way. You want to take a bath while we wait for it?"

"Dinner?" Ryan pushes himself to sitting. "What time is it?"

"Dinnertime," Jesse answers.

Ryan snorts and grabs his phone from the side table and looks at it. "I can't believe I slept all day. Did you sleep, too?"

"Nah, I'm not the one with the busted elbow. Speaking of which, you have an appointment for an X-ray tomorrow morning. I already booked a taxi to take us, and we're getting a new rental after that. The other car's been towed to a local body shop. I contacted my insurance company and they're taking care of it. I paid the tow truck driver extra to bring us your bag and guitar—they're in the living room. Oh, and we were running low on ibuprofen, so I ordered a grocery delivery. It should be here soon."

Ryan looks slightly stunned. "You did all of that while I was asleep?"

"What, you didn't think I was going to spend the whole time creepily staring at you, did you?"

Ryan cracks a smile. "Guess not. Well, is there anything left for me to do?"

"Yeah, one thing."

"What's that?"

"Kiss me."

Ryan's smile softens. He reaches up with his left hand and cups Jesse's chin, drawing him in for a long, slow, only slightly sleep-sour kiss. Jesse sighs and can't believe he's known Ryan for six years and he's only had one day's worth of kissing him. His heart hurts wishing he'd let himself see this as a possibility sooner. How sad would his life have been if he hadn't figured this out?

"Hey, you okay?" Ryan asks, pulling back.

"Yeah. I'm just so fucking glad you gave me a chance to get here," Jesse says.

"Me too." Ryan's eyes look glassy for a second before he blinks the sheen away. "I'm not going to lie and say the last few months haven't been hard. But I really don't want to think about the past anymore. We have so many things to look forward to. So many firsts."

"And second firsts?"

"Yeah." Ryan kisses him again. "If I take a bath, will you join me?"

Jesse's groin tightens at the idea of getting naked with Ryan, even if it's just to take a bath in the huge soaking tub. But he's determined not to mess things up by moving too fast. He pats Ryan's shoulder and eases himself off the bed. "Someone's gotta answer the door when the food comes. But I'll get the bath started for you."

He turns on the taps above the enormous tub in the bathroom adjoining his bedroom. He hopes the grocery order he made gets here before Ryan gets out. He'd ordered Epsom salts, which he wants to add to the water to help with Ryan's stiff muscles. He makes sure there's a washcloth, body wash, and a towel nearby, so Ryan won't have to strain himself to reach anything. He dims the lights over the vanity, turns around to call Ryan in, but the words die in his throat.

Ryan must have performed some truly acrobatic maneuvers to get his clothes off one-handed, but somehow he did it because he's standing in the doorway completely naked. He's even got the sling off, though he's holding his injured elbow carefully against his side. The lamp in the bedroom backlights him, accentuating his lightly muscled shoulders, the trim lines of his waist and hips, leading to strong thighs and calves. Even his feet are sexy.

Jesse's mouth is so dry seeing Ryan entirely nude for the first time that he has to try a couple of times to speak. "Uh. Ready for the bath?" He'd tried to avoid looking at Ryan's crotch, but now his gaze falls helplessly on his dick, thick and growing thicker under Jesse's gaze. Of course Ryan's cock would be as pretty as the rest of him, along with his neatly trimmed thatch of dark brown pubic hair, balanced by the tantalizing weight of his balls.

Ryan walks in and stops by the tub. "You sure you don't want to join me?" His voice is deep and the suggestion in it goes straight to Jesse's own dick, which is extremely interested in what Ryan's offering. He takes a slight step back, as if that'll help him avoid temptation.

"I can't," Jesse says, his voice embarrassingly breathy.

"You don't want to?" Ryan's brow wrinkles in a way that Jesse interprets as slightly hurt. That won't do.

"Ryan, there's literally nothing in the world I want more than to get in that bath with you, but we have to be careful."

"Huh?" Now Ryan just looks confused.

"You know, your arm, and uh, moving too fast, and the delivery people and all that..." Jesse trails off as Ryan steps slowly over the rim of the tub using the grab bar in the wall for leverage. It causes his ass to flex and bunch appealingly before he slides into the water.

"You would never hurt me," Ryan says conversationally. "And there is such a thing as a robe if the delivery comes while we're in here. But if you really don't want to do this now, we can wait."

Jesse's unbuttoning his shirt before Ryan stops talking. He thinks he sees a satisfied look cross Ryan's face before he gets his over shirt off and whips his tee over his head. Socks, belt, jeans follow quickly. His boxer briefs are the only item left, and his thumbs hover over the waistband. It's not that he doesn't want to do this. He so, so does. But Ryan's so...perfect. Ryan's the one whose angel face and unforgettable voice sold his first record. Jesse's just a poser who does a lot of pull-ups.

"What's wrong? The water feels amazing," Ryan says. "And there's plenty of room."

Jesse's saved from answering by a knock on the

cabin's door. He flashes Ryan an apologetic smile, grabs the lodge-provided robe from the wall hook, and escapes.

Columbia apparently only has one delivery person, because the man on the doorstep has two bags of groceries and Jesse's order from the Asian fusion place. Jesse tipped on the app, but he hands over a large denomination bill for good measure, and the delivery guy's face creases with a smile.

"Have a good night," the guy says, and Jesse quietly closes the door. He puts the takeout on the counter in the kitchenette, the perishables in the fridge. He sorts a few of the items into one of the paper bags, and when he's put it off long enough, he takes the bag to the bathroom.

Ryan's washing his hair as best he can with one hand, and Jesse curses himself. He sets the bag down, drops to his knees on the thick bath mat next to the tub.

"Let me help," he says, nudging Ryan's hand away. Ryan relaxes into Jesse's touch as he massages the soap more evenly over Ryan's head, his light brown hair turned darker by the water. He focuses on his task, using his hands to ladle water over Ryan's head to rinse away the suds. When he's done and Ryan's hair is clean, he grabs the washcloth and wipes away some stray bubbles from Ryan's forehead. "All set."

"What's in the bag?" Ryan asks.

"Oh, the Epsom salts. Let me add some and you can keep soaking while I plate up dinner. It came along with the groceries."

Jesse stands up, finds the bag of salt and tears it open, pouring a quarter of the bag into the water.

"Wait, I thought you were going to get in with me?" Ryan sticks his bottom lip out in a slight pout.

"Next time," Jesse says. "You relax, and I'll come back to help you out in a few minutes."

"I can get out of the bathtub by my damn self," Ryan says, but without heat.

"I know you can, but I want to help."

"Okay." Ryan relaxes, closes his eyes. "Don't think I'm going to let you off the hook."

"What do you mean?"

"There's something going on with you. And I'm choosing not to freak out over the possibility that you're regretting this, but I really wish you would just tell me what it is rather than me spinning out bad scenarios in my head."

That stops Jesse in his tracks. Ryan's eyes are still closed, his posture is lax. But he's got a tell, the groove between his eyes, as if he's enduring some phantom pain. Jesse hates that he's the cause of it. As quietly as he can, he shrugs out of the robe, slips off his underwear. He steps into the tub between Ryan's splayed open legs, lowers himself in with care not to jostle Ryan's arm or spill water over the side. Surprisingly, there's room for both of them, two over-six-foot men, if Jesse folds his legs so his knees stick out of the water.

Ryan doesn't open his eyes until Jesse lightly touches the divot in his lip with his forefinger.

"I'm in love with you, Ryan, I'm certain of it. But I haven't been someone's boyfriend in a very long time. I'm out of practice, and I've got to be honest, it's a little intimidating to have to up my game when you're so incredible, and I'm just...regular."

"What do you mean, regular?" Ryan frowns.

"You know. I'm just dorky Jesse Arlyn. But you're *Ryan Winslow*."

"Sorry, I really, really don't understand what you're saying."

Jesse huffs out an impatient breath. "Before I met you, I knew your face. I knew your voice. I was just one fanboy out of hundreds. Thousands. And after I met you, and I got to know you, I only liked you more. But I'm just a kid who joined the Peace Corps because he couldn't make it in music. You're the real star, Ryan. I'm just a satellite orbiting you. And I'm okay with that. But I guess I'm a little scared that you'll wake up one day and realize I'm not that special."

"First of all, you may not have been anyone's boyfriend in a while, but you already know how to be a great partner. You already know how to take care of me. You've taken better care of me than anyone else I've ever known, up to and including my mama. So what if we don't get all this relationship stuff right the first time? We'll figure it out together, okay?"

Jesse smiles a little. He does know how to take care of Ryan. It's pretty much his default mode, and now he can indulge himself all he wants.

"Okay," he answers quietly.

"Second of all, I'm not going to sit here and stroke your ego about how many fan letters you get and how many Grammys you'll have on your shelf someday and how my career would long since have been over if I hadn't met you, because none of that even matters. What matters is that when it's just you and me, just us, you know that I know you're awesome. And if I'm as awesome as you say, then I must be right about how awesome you are. So you can just take that inferiority complex and send it packing. Okay?"

Jesse's pretty sure he follows that logic, or at least he agrees with the part about Ryan being awesome, so he nods. "Sorry. I'm being stupid. Again."

"Good thing I love you, stupid or not."

Jesse's heart feels like it's bobbing in the water, buoyant and light. He grins. "Good thing."

"And I'm not going to push, but I think we need to rip the band aid off. We'll both feel better."

"What band aid?"

"Sex. We need to have sex. Let's just get it over with. How bad can it be?"

Jesse's pretty sure Ryan's joking, but his smile fades. "I just—"

"Look, this morning you promised me an orgasm. Was that a lie?"

"No, but—"

"So I'll make you a deal," Ryan says slyly. "You get me off, but you don't have to come if you don't want to."

Jesse lets out a laugh at that. The idea of touching Ryan, of bringing him to orgasm and not wanting to come himself is patently laughable. Ryan's right, maybe they do just need to rip the band aid off. Though he's fairly certain the process will be more enjoyable than the metaphor implies.

"Okay, fair's fair. I did promise you an orgasm, and I

always keep my promises," Jesse says. "But not in the bath."

Ryan stands up faster than he should be able to with one working arm. "Done."

Jesse, anticipation buzzing in his gut, reaches for a towel.

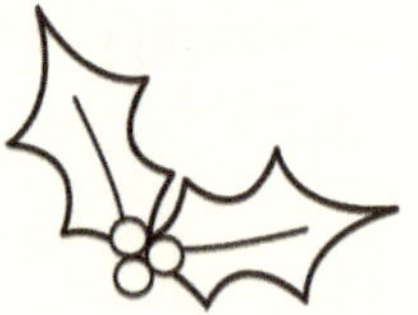

RYAN'S HUNGRY, and a little thirsty, and he's no doubt due for some more pain meds, but nothing is going to stop him from getting Jesse's hands on him. He dries off quickly, returns to the bedroom, and has a terrible thought.

He does an about-face and nearly runs into Jesse coming out of the bathroom, a towel wrapped around his narrow waist.

"I didn't bring any condoms," Ryan says. "I know we don't necessarily need them, but—" To his consternation, Jesse turns around and walks back into the bathroom without answering.

Ryan sighs. He thought he'd convinced his boyfriend to take him to bed, but maybe he needs to work on his game. Jesse's turning out to be a lot less easy, for lack of a better word, than Ryan expected.

Not that he doesn't understand the nerves. What they're embarking on is different from any other relationship Ryan's ever had. They have years of one type of intimacy built up, and all of a sudden they're leaping into an entirely new category. They're bound to have to make adjustments, have a few misunderstandings and false starts. But Jesse's smoking hot, and Ryan wants him so badly. And from the way Jesse's been looking at him all day, touching and kissing him, it's not as if Jesse thinks he's repulsive.

So why is he standing naked in a bedroom alone?

Jesse comes out of the bathroom holding a box of condoms and a bottle of lube.

"I ordered them along with the Epsom salts," he says, shrugging. "Just in case."

"You're a genius," Ryan says, before launching himself at Jesse. He leans up to kiss him, and his elbow gives a twinge. He groans. "This arm is a real spoilsport."

"Here." Jesse puts his offerings down on the table next to the bed, then smooths back the covers. "Lie down, get your arm comfy, and let me keep my promise."

"Yeah?" This is more like it. Ryan does as he's told, settling onto the cool sheets, propping up his arm on an extra pillow.

Jesse sits down next to him. His skin is smooth and there's so much of it. His chest is appealingly dusted with dark wiry hairs. Ryan reaches up to touch, and Jesse lowers himself down so it's easier for him. Then he starts kissing Ryan, but not on the mouth. No, he starts at the hinge of his jaw. Ryan shivers at the sensation. He kisses Ryan's ear, and his neck, his collarbone, a nipple. His tongue flicks the tiny nub and Ryan shivers again, his nipples both standing to attention, waiting for Jesse to do whatever he wants to them.

What Jesse wants is to tease, apparently, licking the other nipple, then returning to Ryan's mouth, which he captures in a deep, open-mouthed kiss that has all the blood in Ryan's body concentrating in his dick.

"Jesse, please," is all Ryan can manage to say before Jesse's moving south, kissing along Ryan's breastbone, down the soft swell of his stomach. He'd be self-conscious about it—he's never had abs of any discernible articulation in his life, not the way Jesse's flat tummy seems to harden into perfectly sexy little ridges when he's shirtless and working out or playing basketball in the driveway of his Austin house. But Jesse doesn't seem to care, just nuzzles Ryan's stomach, kissing his way to his hip bones, until he's so close to Ryan's aching dick he can feel Jesse's warm breath ghosting over it.

"Come on, Jess, you're killing me," Ryan says, aware of the distinct note of begging in his voice and unable to care.

"Gonna make it so good, Ryan," Jesse says, then he pulls back. Ryan wants to cry with frustration, but Jesse goes for the lube. He drizzles some into his hand, holds it for a moment as he looks at Ryan. Ryan's confused, until he realizes Jesse's warming it up. God, he's got the best boyfriend in the world.

"You're really fucking hot," Jesse says while they wait.

"You are, too." Ryan realizes Jesse's still got a towel around his waist and though he'd gotten a glimpse of him naked in the bathroom, he's never seen Jesse hard. "You want to lose the towel?"

"This is about you."

"While I love that sentiment, I really, really want to see you," Ryan says. "Please?" He puffs out his lips in a way that's been known to get Jesse to do what he wants in the past. Jesse rolls his eyes and uses a single finger to flick open the towel, which falls onto the bed, revealing the thick line of Jesse's erection jutting out from dark curls. It bobs a little as Ryan watches, and he suddenly realizes that Jesse's not fully hard yet. He's not sure how much more Jesse has to go, but either way, his boyfriend is a monster. Ryan swallows slightly nervously. "Um."

"Something the matter?" Jesse murmurs as he slowly, firmly, and expertly wraps his slick palm around Ryan's shaft and starts to stroke.

It takes Ryan a minute to find words among all the pleasure signals his brain is putting out. "Gah—no. All. Good." Wet, slick, hot pressure from Jesse's big hands, his cock being confidently stroked, his balls being tugged deliciously, and he's ready to throw his head back and come thirty seconds into the Jesse Arlyn hand job experience.

Jesse chuckles, increases his speed. "That's right. Just feel good for me, darlin'. There are so many ways I'm going to make you feel good. This is just the start. I'm going to blow you. I'm going to fuck you." Jesse touches Ryan's hole with one hot, slippery finger, and Ryan bites his lip hard to keep from coming right that instant.

"Is that something you want?" Jesse asks, rubbing at Ryan's entrance firmly but not penetrating him. "Have you thought about me fucking you, Ryan?"

Ryan moans, overstimulated and yet Jesse's not jacking him hard enough to make him come. Jesse stops his motions entirely. "Have you thought about it, darlin'?" Jesse asks again, his voice deceptively soft. "Thought about me filling you up with my cock?"

He nods, gaze glued to where Jesse's hand is wrapped around his shaft, willing him to start moving it again.

"Tell me what you thought about."

Words? Jesse expects him to be able to come up with words at a time like this? "Uh. Thought about getting in your lap. About, uh, sitting on your cock."

Jesse's hand twitches, squeezing him reflexively, and he starts stroking again, as if rewarding Ryan for what he'd said. "Yeah? You want to sit down on my big cock?"

"Didn't know it was quite, uh, that big," Ryan admits.

"It's okay. I'll get you nice and open," Jesse promises. "You won't have any trouble taking me when I'm through with you."

"Oh fuck." If Ryan thought he couldn't be any more in love with Jesse, he'd just have been proven wrong. He's not hung up on size, but if he's being honest, he's always preferred a bigger package.

Jesse starts circling Ryan's hole with his finger even as he continues to jack him with steady pressure. "I'll make sure you're so ready for me, darlin'. I'll have you open and ready to get filled up. You can sink right down on me until you feel me in the back of your throat. It's going to be so incredible, Ryan, you don't even know."

He pushes through the tight ring of muscle with one finger, the finger he uses to make beautiful music on the guitar, and Ryan disintegrates with pleasure, the sharp intrusion combined with the grip on his cock and the dirty promise in Jesse's voice all pushing him into an explosive orgasm he can feel rattling his molars and curling his toes.

He thrashes and yells and feels come rapidly cooling on his stomach. When the pleasure subsides to a tolerable level, he opens his eyes. Jesse's scooping fluid off Ryan's belly, then reaching down to grasp his own cock.

"Let me see," Ryan orders with the last of his strength. Jesse shifts so Ryan can see his thick, long shaft disappearing and reappearing in the channel made by his hand, the way slicked by a little lube and Ryan's jizz. "Yeah. Fuck, Jesse. So fucking hot. You made it so fucking good for me. I want you to do that. I want you to open me up and push me down on your cock. I'm going to take it so good, I swear—"

And Jesse's coming, a deep groan wrenching from his chest, globs of come spilling between his fingers.

When they both have their breath back, and Jesse's wiped them down with a wet washcloth retrieved from the bathroom, Ryan almost feels like he could crawl right back under the covers and back to sleep. Then he hears a familiar gurgle. Jesse's stomach making its hunger known. He laughs.

"Dinnertime?" he asks.

Jesse grins. "I don't know about you, but I worked up an appetite."

"You definitely earned your keep," Ryan agrees. He makes himself sit up, kisses his boyfriend.

Jesse looks pleased, grabs them some underwear and

pajama pants. "You want to stay here? I can bring you food."

"That actually sounds amazing. Thanks. But let me ask one thing first."

"Go for it."

"Glad we ripped off the band aid?"

Jesse nods, his eyes soft to match the set of his mouth. "It didn't hurt a bit."

LATER, after they've eaten, and talked, and cuddled a little, Ryan's nestled into Jesse's embrace, unselfconscious about the closeness even though it usually takes him a while to get comfortable sharing his space with guys. But Jesse's not any other guy. Jesse is *the* guy. The only guy for Ryan.

"What are we going to do about Christmas?" Jesse asks.

"What do you mean?"

"Well, our families are expecting us to come home."

"Is that not the plan?"

"But your arm—"

"I can travel with it. We can't stay here forever," Ryan says, though he kind of wishes they could.

"I guess we'll have to put the album on the back burner for a while."

"Our non-corny Christmas album?"

"Yeah. Oh well. We'll finish it sometime."

"I have a love song to add to it," Ryan says, thinking of his song for Jesse.

"As a matter of fact, I do, too," Jesse says.

"What do you mean?"

"Last night, I was writing you a song to convince you to stay. To convince you to give me another chance, but I got sidetracked by the snow and you thinking the laws of physics don't apply to you."

"Well, let's hear it then," Ryan says. He loves Jesse's songs, and he gets a little thrill knowing Jesse wrote one with him specifically in mind.

"It's not ready yet," Jesse says.

"Please? I need a lullaby to get me to sleep," Ryan whines.

"God, you're a brat," Jesse says, planting a kiss on the top of Ryan's head. "Okay. I have to get my guitar."

Ryan wriggles happily while he waits for the love of his life to serenade him.

Jesse returns a minute later, tuning his guitar lightly. He sits on the edge of the bed, wearing nothing but a pair of soft gray pajama pants. His dark hair hangs in his face, and he has a red mark on his neck that Ryan put there with his mouth.

"You're so beautiful," Ryan says.

"Hush," Jesse says lightly. "Promise you'll go to sleep after this?"

"Yes. Well, after this and after I brush my teeth."

Jesse snorts and starts to play. The tune is slow at first, dreamy country chords that Jesse matches with his soulful voice. He doesn't have as much range as Ryan, but he's got a compelling baritone twang.

> *I promised I wouldn't write*
> *another corny Christmas song.*

> *I promised you there'd be snow.*
> *I promised myself I'd never fall in love,*
> *but, baby, wouldn't you just know?*

Ryan smiles as Jesse catalogs his failed promises, and then the tempo picks up and Jesse sings on.

> *It turns out I'm a liar.*
> *And not a good one at that.*
> *'Cause feet to the fire,*
> *you laid me out flat.*
>
> *I fell for your voice,*
> *your heart, and your mind.*
> *The way you smile when I'm being*
> *   foolish,*
> *the way our lives are entwined.*
>
> *I saved your life*
> *way back when.*
> *But you've saved mine*
> *over and over again.*
>
> *Please say it's not too late.*
> *Please tell me I got one more chance.*
> *To prove ours is a love*
> *that's gonna last and last.*
>
> *There's not much Christmas*
> *in this corny Christmas song.*
> *So let's find some mistletoe*

and kiss our whole lives long.

Ryan's smiling through his tears when Jesse finally sets the guitar to the side. "I love it, Jess," he says. "It's my new favorite Christmas song."

"Yeah?" Jesse's smile is the best Christmas present Ryan could ask for. "Well, I mean every word."

"Then there's only one thing left to do," Ryan says, pulling Jesse in close. "We better find some mistletoe."

They kiss as if the entire ceiling is covered in the stuff.

EPILOGUE

Four months later

"ARE you absolutely sure those are the ticket totals?" Hank asks for the third time since Emma made the calculations.

Emma rolls her eyes at her brother. "Yes, Hank. In person ticket sales alone are going to get us past our goal. With the online streaming revenue and the merchandise sales, the clinic is going to be in great shape for a long time to come."

"I knew Jesse and Ryan were successful, but I had no idea they were this popular," Hank says, a little dazed.

"That's because your idea of contemporary music is Dave Matthews Band, babe," Cameron says, softening the blow by slipping his hand into Hank's back pocket and giving his ass a light squeeze.

"It is not. I like, um," he racks his brain for a more recent artist, "Garth Brooks."

"Garth is a legend, but you're kind proving my

point." Cameron laughs and removes his hand. "I gotta go to work. See you after?"

Hank grins at his boyfriend. "See you after."

Except for a couple of gigs Cameron already had scheduled, he's basically been living in Columbia since before Christmas. At first, he was recuperating from his big tour, and then just when Hank had assumed their holiday fling would be ending and Cameron would go back to his life, Emma had mentioned their idea for a fundraiser for the clinic and Cameron had jumped on it, declaring that he would produce it and take care of everything.

Somewhere in there, Hank realized he was dreading the moment when Cameron told him it would be time to say goodbye. When he got up the courage to tell him just that, Cameron had smiled and said, "I hope I never have to say goodbye to you." Whether Cameron ends up on tour again or not, Hank knows that they'll figure things out.

The last month has been a whirlwind of activity. First, the tickets went on sale for an intimate show featuring Jesse Arlyn, Ryan Winslow, and Cameron Keane, and it sold out in about five minutes, so they added two more shows and those sold out, too. They've converted the lodge's great room into a concert space for the weekend. Emma used the event as an excuse to fast track some property upgrades, and Cameron took charge of sprucing up the baby grand piano that was a relic of Hank's grandparents' days. Workers have been in and out all week installing lights, a sound system, and a temporary stage. Jesse and Ryan arrived a couple of days ago for rehearsals. Hank had wanted to put them up in cabin 12, unofficially the honeymoon suite, but they'd requested cabin 14 again. Something about the bathtub. Hank hadn't asked too many questions.

After all the planning, Hank's excited for the show to begin. Emma sends him back to his place to get dressed. He trims his beard and combs his hair and puts on a new black button-down shirt, tucks it into his nicest jeans. Cameron and Jesse and Ryan are the ones with the spotlight on them tonight, but he wants to do them proud. After all, they've gone to all this trouble for the clinic when it's not their responsibility. He gets a little emotional when he thinks about how much they've all grown up, how they've all met the challenges of the world in different ways. He's proud of Jesse and Ryan, good men who haven't forgotten that their fame and influence can do a lot of good in the world.

Emma collects him a little before the show's supposed to start. She looks radiant in a snow-white sweater and black jeans. "Ready?"

"I'm weirdly nervous," Hank admits.

"Everything is running like clockwork. They're professionals. Just let them do their thing and you enjoy the show."

"Thanks, sis." They're at the side entrance when Hank hears the strains of one of Ryan's songs start up and the crowd goes wild. When he and Emma get inside and head for their reserved seats, he can see how packed it is with people seated in the front and standing in the back. Some backup musician friends of Ryan and Jesse's are already on stage. Then Cameron takes the stage, settling behind the refurbished grand piano, and there's a fresh round of cheers. Cameron finds Hank in the crowd and winks. Hank shouldn't be flustered like a teenager with his first crush, but somehow he's blushing beneath his beard anyway.

Then Jesse and Ryan bound onto the stage, waving to the crowd that greets them like they're the Beatles or something. It's wild. Hank's cheeks already ache from smiling so hard and they haven't even played a single song yet.

But that deficiency is remedied right away as they launch into one of their big hits. The crowd is instantly into it, and even Emma starts singing along with the chorus. Hank glances at her.

"What? I like this song," she says.

He shrugs and takes it all in, the effortless chemistry between Jesse and Ryan on stage, the way they have command of their instruments, the intimacy of their voices in the relatively small space. Jesse, for sure, seems to love the energy coming off the crowd and seems more willing to look out and interact with the audience, while Ryan seems more focused on his guitar. When he's not focused on Jesse, that is. They can't seem to keep their eyes off each other for more than thirty seconds at a time, constantly tracking the other, tuned in to each other, literally.

Hank enjoys watching Cameron, too. He hasn't had many chances to see him perform for a crowd, and it's clear he's a pro from the way he can manage to play, sing, and interact with the other band members all at once. Hank never understood the whole "musicians are hot" thing fully until right this very moment. He wants to drag Cameron off that stage and take him to bed, damn the rest of the concert.

But he's got more self-control than that.

They finish a song, and Ryan takes over the center mic. He waits for the screams and applause to die down, then says, "We're here tonight to raise money for a really worthy cause, the Columbia Health Clinic. Every penny we make is going to expand access to healthcare for the good people of this part of Vermont and we're so grateful to everyone for showing up tonight to be a part of that. Access to healthcare is something Jesse and I care a lot about, so we're also donating the proceeds from our next album to that effort. It's called *Another Corny Christmas Album*, it's coming your way later this year, and we're working on it right now. It's been Christmas every day for us lately, hasn't it, Jess?"

Jesse steps up to the mic. "That's right, Ryan. We've been very much in the spirit of giving, especially since reconnecting with our old friend and Peace Corps buddy, Dr. Hank Moore. Give it up for Hank, everybody!"

Suddenly, a spotlight swivels to light him up. Hank feels very exposed, while the entire crowd hollers at Jesse's urging. He kind of wants to hide behind Emma, but instead he waves and the crowd cheers again.

"Hank's not only the best doctor in Vermont, he's also an owner of Pine Tree Lodge. He grew up here, and he and his sister still run it. It's a special place, and it holds a special place in my and Ryan's hearts," Jesse goes on. "Hank was there when I first met Ryan, and he helped us through some tough times more recently. He's the best guy I know, a true friend, and an inspiration to me and Ryan to try to be the best versions of ourselves every day. So thanks, Hank. We love you." Jesse looks right at him and smiles.

Jesse goes blurry as Hank blinks away tears. He nods. Jesse and Ryan know he loves them, too.

"So in the spirit of love, friendship, and all that good stuff, we thought we might play a new song for you. Wanna hear it?"

The crowd goes absolutely bananas, and Jesse chuckles into the mic. "That's what I thought. Ryan, you wanna say a little something about this song?"

Ryan clears his throat. "Yeah. I wrote this song when I was trying to tell a certain tall drink of water how I felt about him." The audience coos. "It didn't exactly have the effect I intended right away. But eventually, he got the message." There's a swell of laughter and Jesse grins self-deprecatingly. "But I kept working on the song, and it'll be on our Christmas album, even though it's not very Christmassy. But it is universal. So I hope you like it. It's called 'An Old-Fashioned Love Song.' Thanks for the title, Hank." Ryan winks at him.

Hank's heart couldn't be fuller.

The song starts with a traditional country twang, and Ryan starts singing, his voice unfurling like cedar smoke. A hush seems to fall on the crowd as they listen. Even Jesse, who's playing guitar, is completely transfixed by Ryan, whose eyes are closed as he sings into the mic.

I wanna be more than friends.

My heart's on the line.
I could be yours
and you could be mine.

My love's not a gift.
Not a spell or a curse.
It's just how I feel
for better or worse.

You're everything to me.
But that's all it has to be.
Could I be everything to you?
Could it be that you want me, too?

I wanna be more than friends.
My heart beats despite its cracks.
I think I'm in love
with someone who loves me back.

I once doubted your love.
I was scared but you stayed true.
Love called us both out.
And we made it through.

Old fashioned it may be.
I love you, I do.
As a friend and a lover
it was always going to be you.

Ryan opens his eyes, and the crowd erupts into earsplitting cheers. Hank's clapping so hard his hands are burning.

They swiftly change gears into something brisk and up tempo, and the energy never goes back down. By the time everyone on stage is taking a final bow, Hank feels like he's run a marathon. He can't imagine how the performers feel. It takes some time for the crowd to disperse. Emma disappears to make sure the security they hired is doing their jobs of getting everyone safely off the property, except for the ones who are paying guests. Hank goes to the kitchen, which has been partially converted to a backstage green room for this event.

People dressed in black are dealing with instruments and equipment, and Cameron and Jesse and Ryan are clustered together, talking over each other excitedly, faces red and sweaty.

"Babe!" Cameron catches sight of him and Hank tackles him in a bear hug.

"That was incredible."

"Good show, right?" Cameron says.

"The crowd loved it," Hank says. "And so did I. But you guys didn't have to say all that stuff."

"We wanted to," Ryan says, clapping him on the shoulder. "And we meant it."

Jesse grins toothily. "Besides, we're still auditioning for the Moore-Keane wedding gig."

"Dude, give us a minute," Cameron says, laughing. "Besides, what about you two? Or are you going to elope and save us the drama?"

Jesse smiles at Ryan. "I don't know. We wouldn't

want to deprive our mamas of a wedding, would we, darlin'?"

"They'd probably kill us if we did, Jess," Ryan agrees happily.

"Wait—you mean?" Cameron goggles at them.

Hank notices for the first time the matching slender gold bands on their ring fingers. "You guys got engaged?"

"Last night," Ryan says, his eyes bright and his smile so wide it looks painful.

There's a fresh round of everyone hugging everyone else as Cameron and Hank congratulate them. Jesse and Ryan put their arms around each other, and Hank can't think of any two people who've ever been more meant to be.

"This calls for champagne." There must be a spare bottle or two in the lodge's wine stores.

"When are you doing the deed?" Cameron asks.

"We haven't really talked about it. Maybe this Christmas?" Ryan suggests.

"Isn't that kind of corny?" Jesse asks. "Mistletoe and snow and all that?"

"It turns out I kinda like corny," Ryan says, looking at Jesse like he's a snow day and Christmas morning and pumpkin pie and eggnog all rolled up into one. "In fact, I love it."

"I love it, too," Jesse says, and then they kiss.

It's the corniest, happiest ending anyone could possibly hope for.

I hope you enjoyed this corny Christmas love story!
For a free feel-good small-town gay romance story, sign
up for my newsletter at
ellewatersbooks.substack.com!

xoxo, Elle

ABOUT THE AUTHOR

Fueled by chocolate and canned wine, Elle Waters writes steamy, feel-good, small town romances with guaranteed happy endings. She lives with her family in Connecticut. Sign up for her newsletter at ellewatersauthor.com to hear about her next release! Elle loves to hear from readers at elle@ellewatersauthor.com.

facebook.com/ElleWatersAuthor

instagram.com/ellewatersbooks

amazon.com/~/e/B091FZQ4PZ

bookbub.com/authors/elle-waters

reamstories.com/ellewaters